Subway to Europe

The attack on
the Channel Tunnel

Subway to Europe

The attack on the Channel Tunnel

Peter Meynell

THE PENTLAND PRESS LIMITED
Edinburgh Cambridge Durham USA

First published in 1996
by Cross Publishing

This edition published
by Pentland Press, 1999

ISBN : 1 85821 699 0

Printed in Great Britain

Author's note

This book is a work of fiction and entertainment based on many facts. The author wrote it to draw attention to the strategic importance of the Channel Tunnel, and to explore its vulnerability by means of fiction.

No characters or events depicted are true, therefore the author and his agents disclaim any and all suggestions that they are real. Purchase or use of this book are conditional that its readers will not construe the story in any way other than as a piece of bedtime reading, with a timely message about the futility of war, the scourge of civilisation for centuries past and present.

The author makes no claim in fact that the tunnel is unsafe, and having travelled through it by shuttle and express train, in great comfort and with immense admiration for its efficiency and convenience, he prefers it to any other method of crossing the Channel, by a very wide margin. It is probably safer than any other tunnel in the world.

Acknowledgments

To my friends Elza and Ben who lived in Mechelen during the degrading years of the Nazi occupation, and although reluctant to discuss the miseries and indignities they suffered - being good Europeans - kindly showed me around their beautiful Belgian countryside on several occasions, knowing that this unforgiving book would be the result. Their wartime suffering made a deep impression.

Subway To Europe

If I have mastery of the Channel for six hours, I have mastery of the world.
Napoleon Bonaparte before Austerlitz

Even if we cannot conquer, we shall drag the world into destruction with us.
Adolf Hitler in Mein Kampf

If we do not face reality, reality will face us.
Winston Churchill

Prologue

FAREWELL TO THE 20TH CENTURY

By the time Hitler's power-crazed, overbearing and sadistic military machine had finished rampaging across Europe and Russia, lying, killing, torturing, pillaging and stealing almost all that remained of the civilised culture that had taken centuries to achieve, and was so nearly extinguished by the Kaiser's Great War, a burning hatred had been rekindled once more, and perhaps may never be extinguished. The thoughts of exacting revenge were kept alive by those who had lost most during the Cold War which followed, and in the hearts of the plotters in this story, many of whom had lost not only parents, homes, possessions and neighbours, sometimes in tragic and usually brutal circumstances, but also their youth and almost all hope as they were goaded, herded and prodded like cattle by the conquerors, who cared little for their miserable plight.

Throughout this Twentieth Century, pain and misery have been suffered by over one hundred million members of the human race who lost their lives by following their leaders blindly, instead of learning that ruin often results from unquestioning trust.

This book is dedicated to a far-fetched hope, that in the 21st Century the people of a more enlightened world will stop their infatuation with oratory and misleading political rhetoric, delivered by ambitious and greedy politicians looking for a privileged career with a comfortable future, at the expense of the less articulate, heavily taxed majority, so that they may truly receive the rewards of their hard toil, tears and sweat.

With the end of the Cold War, the forces of East and West on the Continent of Europe found themselves closely matched militarily, if not ideologically. The impasse meant that the Slav nations could not exact revenge for the tragedies of the past. But this changed when far-sighted Comrade Mikhail Gorbachev rode to the rescue, and his successors lulled the NATO partners into reducing their powerful military forces stationed on the Continent.

The Soviet old guard, never eradicated and often fêted from Moscow in the west to Yakutsk in the east, could see that their time had come again, not just to threaten the West but possibly to succeed where even Comrade Joseph Stalin had failed, in the classic Russian roulette game of European military chess.

2

The clash of computers, long predicted by the French controller at the Calais Terminal, was happening with frightening rapidity. The phone lines alongside the computer terminals at Folkestone and Calais were continually jammed as the controllers at Folkestone fought to maintain an orderly transfer of powers to Calais.

"Jean, I will have to push my red button if you are ready - we can't go on like this." George Trent, the Controller West, spoke in an agitated voice to his opposite number, as he realised that the armed attack on the tunnel might succeed unless Calais took control. The alarms had sounded, a fire had started in the shuttle train inside the tunnel, and the automatic train control system had halted the shuttle at an access point where police and fire-fighters could intercept it via the service tunnel between the two tracks.

"George, I will send my special police force in from this end. The train is only five kilometres into the tunnel."

"OK, Jean, will you do that as soon as you can? Now, will you take over control?"

"Yes, hand over now George."

The Controller West pressed the red button, but nothing happened.

"Jean, there is a power failure, according to our computers. Our screens have gone blank. Have you got the same problem?"

There was no reply.

CHAPTER 1

The Eurotunnel Terminal at Folkestone

As the brilliant blue and white helicopter carrying the Transport Minister wheeled over the enormous Eurotunnel Terminal at Folkestone, a dark grey cloud billowed up from the ground below.

"What on earth is that?" shouted the Minister over the intercom. He looked down anxiously, as the helicopter rocked.

"Nothing to worry about, Minister. We are having a photo opportunity for the Press down there," said George Trent, the Controller West, over the intercom. "The real explosion would be a lot more dramatic. We are showing the media how we search and blow up suspect vehicles. That smoke came up from the Terminator. It's an enclosed area where freight lorries which fail their X-ray test go for their last journey. We can't be too careful, can we?" The Controller was thinking of the international terrorist network, Her Majesty's enemies, the Eurotunnel balance sheet, and many other distractions, like the Minister's visit.

"Well, obviously the Government supports any measures you take to protect the tunnel, as they safeguard our vital link with the Continent, but that looked a bit close. By the way, George, I trust we won't have to meet the Press today. They have a habit of asking weird questions, like how much money did the Government contribute to the Tunnel. They seldom ask intelligent questions, in my opinion. We never did offer to finance this hole in the ground, if you will pardon the expression. It would have taken longer and cost more that way."

The minister had spoken glibly, and Trent was not amused.

"No, we don't let them into the Control Centre - its security is absolute. We just wanted them to see the Terminator today. They are always trying to come here." The two men flew on past the Control Centre and the four huge concrete overbridges, towards the tunnel portal at the east end of the terminal.

"Tell me George, why do you need four overbridges?" asked the Minister. Trent shut off the intercom and groaned. The Minister hailed from Merthyr Tydfil in the Welsh valleys, where bridges were in short supply.

"Did you come to the opening ceremony in 1994? I thought you were there. We have to load the eastbound shuttles going to France from two overbridges, one for the front of the train and one for the rear. There are twenty-eight wagons in a shuttle, and it would take half an hour if we used only one loading bridge. The same with the shuttles arriving from France: we use two to unload; one for the front and one for the rear of the train."

"Yes, I remember, but it does seem a vast set-up to cater for just two tunnels."

"It may look that way, but some trains, such as freight and express, go straight through and don't use the shuttle system, so they arrive on separate tracks. That's why it looks more complicated than it is."

"You know, the view from the air is amazing, isn't it?" said the Minister, as the helicopter swung round in front of the white entrance portals, ready to plane back down to the helipad. He wished he could have been responsible for this colossal feat of engineering..

"Well, it has been described as the project of the century, Minister, and is certainly the largest construction project ever undertaken, except for the Great Wall of China - but that took nearly two thousand years to complete, and we had to build this tunnel in six years."

The helicopter banked steeply over the white Control Centre building, and swooped down onto the helipad. A figure came out to greet them, dodging the whirling blades with his head and body bent low.

"That's my Deputy Controller, Jack Holmes," said Trent. "He's more of a Watson than a Holmes, but he runs the Control Centre, and he will show you to your seat before the security seminar begins."

The two men stepped out of the machine with heads bowed as the helicopter's engine whined to a halt and the rotor stopped, then exchanged brief greetings with Holmes. He guided them quickly into the Centre, and to their seats in front of the enormous lighted control panel inside. Trent walked up to the lectern and addressed the waiting audience.

"Ladies and gentlemen, may I welcome on your behalf the Transport Minister, the Right Honourable Ivor Williams MP, who has come here today in order to find out how we protect the Tunnel from subversion and other security problems. Now you, the invited audience, will be able to play a full part in this seminar. The panel is made up of senior staff from the terminal, and also some of the French staff from Calais terminal. We are most grateful for their presence here today, in particular my opposite number, the Controller East, Monsieur Jean Moris. Our audience includes several members of the general public, who obviously want to know how safe it is to travel under the English Channel, and includes selected Sixth Form students from St Michael's School, Folkestone, who have been busy rehearsing their questions to address to the panel. But before we start the questions, there will be a short presentation by my Deputy, Jack Holmes, on the workings of the rail control indicator display." The Minister by now seemed to have difficulty in staying awake: it had been a hard night. He dimly heard a few more words before relapsing into a state of apparent limbo.

"Good morning gentlemen. In front of you here we have, stretching for twenty-four metres from left to right, the Rail Control Display. This indicates, around the clock, all the rail activities at this terminal, in the tunnel itself, and at the Calais terminal. It is larger and more complex than the layout at the Space Centre in Houston, Texas. All rail movements including those at Calais are shown and controlled from here, and it would only be in an emergency that control would pass to the Calais control centre, which is similar to this one." The Minister dozed on, hoping that nobody would ask him anything.

"The terminal platforms are shown in green, yellow is used for the rail tracks, and red is only used for an accident or emergency such as a fire. The two banks of computers in front of you are connected to all the different parts of the system so that we can zoom in on any trouble spot, or check up on what is happening anywhere in the rail system." A deathly hush had fallen on the assembled audience as the Minister seemed to grunt audibly.

"From this control centre we can communicate verbally and often visually with most parts of the Eurotunnel network, from the passenger terminals, arrivals areas, platforms and loading bridges, and to all trains travelling between the two terminals in England and France. If we get an indication that there is a problem with one of the trains, we can take over the driving from this terminal. In case you think we are working in the dark here, on the upper floor of the centre, above your heads, there is another team operating visually by looking out of the panoramic windows and keeping a round-the-clock watch on activity at the terminal outside.

"Now, here we have some sparkling white lights on the indicator, which show us that a train has just come through the tunnel. The indicator shows UEBW, which means the Up Express from Brussels to Waterloo. That was well timed, and we can also see some activity at the Shuttle loading area at the east end of the Terminal. The indicator shows DSFC, which means the Down Shuttle from Folkestone to Calais. I can call up the platform via this computer and get an instant report" - here Mr Holmes pressed a few keys and spoke to the platform. "Yes, they confirm fifteen more heavy goods vehicles to be loaded and departure in ten minutes, as scheduled. Now, after that short introduction, may we have the first question from the audience?" The Minister tried vainly to keep awake.

"Richard Snow, Sixth Form, St Michael's Folkestone. I would like to ask the panel this question: If I tried to bring a bomb into the Channel Tunnel, how could you stop me?"

The Controller West suppressed a yawn himself - the question had been put to him so many times before. He did not really know all the answers. "Perhaps the Chief Security Officer Folkestone would like to reply to that one?"

"Yes, certainly." Mr Charles Sleight stood up to reply. "Of course our actions would depend on which way you were travelling, or in other words how the bomb was being carried - by heavy goods vehicle, passenger car or coach on the Shuttle wagons, by freight train, or as a passenger on the Eurostar high speed express train from Waterloo. I should explain that we have a separate security centre elsewhere in the terminal area to monitor access and security in the tunnel. We begin by searching every vehicle and every piece of luggage before it can enter the tunnel. This is like an airline check-in, but we make sure it is even more extensive and thorough. If there is any suspicion at all, then access to the train is barred, and a fuller investigation takes place. If we have doubts, we blow up the suspected baggage, load or vehicle - as the Minister already knows, having flown over the Terminator demolition area on his way here this morning. We invited the Press and TV to see the Terminator today so that the public will know what happens to any suspicious object sent into the terminal." The Minister stirred slightly, at the mention of his title, and even tried to look alert in case a question was put to him.

"Next question to the panel - any member of the audience?"

"David Howard, Railtrack South East. Can the panel describe what steps are taken to prevent unauthorised train movements or stoppages in the tunnel?"

"Perhaps the Rail Traffic Manager will answer that?" Holmes was fully in charge again, after the setback of seeing the Minister almost fast asleep.

"Yes, I'm John Hume, Traffic Manager. As you have already seen, we have visual presentation of all rail movements from this control centre, and can over-ride the actions of the train drivers themselves, both in the UK terminal and at Calais. The system was developed for the French TGV high speed trains and incorporates a series of fail-safe procedures to prevent any unauthorised activities. If for example the train driver takes his foot off the Vacmar - the foot pedal which controls the power supply - our computer takes over the running of the train until the driver calls to say he is fit to take over. If a bomb went off on a train, we could split the train and leave the damaged portion behind to be dealt with from the service tunnel. With an engine at both ends we could of course take out undamaged parts of the train. I might add that the tunnel is designed to be bomb-proof, and the concrete lining is the strongest that has ever been used - twice as strong as the material used in a nuclear reactor."

"Speaking about nuclear matters, are you saying that a nuclear weapon could not destroy the tunnel? I am Harold Cartwright, Atomic Energy Authority."

"I can say with some certainty that not only could a radio-active device be detected before it got into the tunnel, because it would be picked up in the screening process - but also might not succeed in seriously damaging the tunnel." There was a murmur of surprise from the audience, and the Minister came to his senses with a start.

"Could I ask a question about power supply in an emergency?" The speaker was standing up. "I'm a scientist at Nuclear Electric, and quite familiar with power networks. My question is: Could the power supply be cut by terrorist action, and if so how could that problem be overcome?"

"Engineering Management, would you answer that one?" Another pretty basic question, the Controller thought to himself.

"Yes, I'm Bob Hoskins, in charge of electric power management. The power comes from either of the national grids, UK or French, via our own sub-station, and although there are 950 kilometres of overhead conductor, or catenary, there is a high degree of redundancy. So if we get a failure at one place we can normally go round the point of failure by electronic control means, and reset the system. It would not be possible to cut out more than 500 metres of the catenary, and this problem could be overcome or the power reinstated within twenty to thirty minutes, at most."

"Are you also saying that you could overcome a major failure at your electricity sub-station?" asked the persistent questioner.

"Yes I am - we could take electric power at 25,000 volts direct from the Calais sub-station if ours failed, and divert it as required."

"May I put a question to our British friends?" Jean Moris, the slim, intellectual French Controller East spoke quietly. A man with an impressive track record at SNCF, the French railway company, he had also served with distinction as a director of one of the five French firms which shared in the tunnel's construction, working with five British firms on the other side of the Channel. He chose his words carefully, as he illuminated where others obscured.

"I sometimes feel that the only security problem we should think about more, is the handover of control from Folkestone to Calais in an emergency. Although our Red Book of procedures covers most likely problems, and our staff are mostly bi-lingual, and we have our famous Police-speak standard language, produced at your Cambridge University for both nationalities to use in emergencies, I think there could still be a failure to communicate or decide the correct course of action in a real, major emergency - and that failure could be very expensive indeed."

"I think I should answer that." George Trent, the Controller West stood up to add emphasis to his words. "We have this very expensive computer system linking the two control systems, and hundreds of miles - or kilometres - of optic fibre connections to pass information all the time, but I agree with our good friend Monsieur Jean Moris." The Minister sat upright at last, listening with more interest. Technical matters were not his bag, but procedural problems were. George Trent continued in his reassuring way.

"We still have to go on practising our co-operation procedures, and if necessary bring more standard procedures into our Red Book system for dealing with emergencies. We both agree on that, and at our monthly conferences we analyse each security exercise carried out here and at Calais. Eventually we must have covered most possibilities, and your questions today will, I am sure, have helped us in our thinking. Minister, I know you have a tiring schedule today, as always, and we must bring this short seminar to a close, but I think we have time for one more question. St Michael's School - I know you have been working on this very hard - one last query on a subject we have not already covered, please."

A tall, slim, bespectacled youth stood up. "Matthew Jones. My question is this: how could the trains continue to function if you lost power throughout the system, not just the power supply to the catenary but also to the terminal facilities such as the Control Centre itself?"

There was a natural pause as the panel and audience pondered the effect of a total failure of the whole power supply to the tunnel system controlled by Folkestone. George Trent spoke, rather slowly and carefully. Security mattered above all, but he had to give a convincing answer.

"Well, first we would restore power to the Control Centre by means of its emergency generators. Then we could use our computers to find out the extent of the failure. If our power station had completely failed, we could import power from the French Electricity grid, as has already been mentioned, but there would be some delay while we checked that power systems were still working - for example, converting the voltage to 25,000 for the tunnel and lower voltages for the terminal operating equipment - by that I mean all the electrical appliances, lighting, signalling and so on. We would expect to be back in business within half an hour or less."

There was a general silence, so the Minister stood up, rather stiffly. "Well, I am sure that will give us something to think about. It has been a very interesting seminar. I suppose quite a lot can happen in half an hour. Anyway, I will leave that thought with Eurotunnel, and thank you all very much for your efforts here today." The Minister was wide awake now, and had begun to ask himself some questions about the long term future of the tunnel after hearing some disturbing facts which were not known to his Department.

As the Minister and Controller left the building together, and walked to the helipad, George Trent felt that the very simple presentation had gone well, but he too was now uneasy about his revelation that the tunnel could be immobilised for so long. He certainly didn't want the Minister to start a scare in Parliament which would spread, and cause a serious threat to revenue, as well as security in the operation of the tunnel.

"I hope, Minister," he said on the way to the helipad, "you realise that the answer to the last question was off the cuff, and we can't reveal all our precautions to the public. In fact my answer was intended to protect security by not going into details - you might say I was misleading the public but the end justifies the means. I can let you have some written answers if you need more facts. We might well recover from a total power failure much more quickly than I indicated."

"No, I don't think there will be any problem until I have spoken to the Cabinet, George - I will be in touch within a week or so. It was, as I said, an interesting seminar, which made me think a bit more about the question of national security - which I could not mention there. It is imperative that in time of war the tunnel is kept open for as long as possible, as it may be the only means of sending reinforcements to Europe - as you are well aware. So if there is a weakness, perhaps in communications, as Monsieur Moris suggested, that is an area that may need looking at again. Perhaps you would keep me informed."

The Controller stood waving goodbye as the helicopter took off and flew the Minister to the floating heliport on the river Thames. It soon disappeared from view. There would be a scene at the Cabinet meeting next Thursday, he thought glumly. The responsibilities of the job began to grow larger every year. First, delays in opening the tunnel, then technical problems, then revenue problems, now security problems. He had always stuck to a firm rule in life: perseverance pays. Don't give up, there must be a solution to every problem - so find it, and don't keep worrying. A man in his mid-fifties, George Trent was the typical modern technocrat. Born in 1945 in North London, named after the King in that great victory year, a product of strict parents, Grammar school, a scholarship to Oxbridge (he had attended both universities), he seemed an ideal choice to head the Channel tunnel control team when Eurotunnel was selecting its man. Tall, thin and intense, he had come from the sharp end of industry, and towered comfortably above the Minister who had come to look at the project of the century from a background in the distant Welsh valleys. Trent suddenly felt vulnerable, but he hurried back to say goodbye to his friend Jean Moris before he left for France on the next shuttle train.

"Jean, I hope you agree that it was not wise to talk about a complete breakdown of the power supply in front of the audience we had today. They did not need to know anything about Project Brunel - don't you think?"

"Yes, I am sure you are right, George, because in reality, we have no hope of Project Brunel being funded, have we? Anyway, we'll keep on trying, *n'est ce pas*? And cheer up, *mon ami*," he smiled. With that the Controller East climbed into his car and drove off to the Shuttle loading bridges, bound for Calais, leaving Trent to worry about what the Minister would do when he got back to London. That was one problem Trent would not be able to solve. He wondered where it might end.

CHAPTER 2

At Mechelen, Near Brussels

At Donkerlei the light was always feeble. The sun had done its best to deliver some brightness to the South side of the dark lane, but it was still too low, and could only reach the grey roof tops of the North side. Number 6 was on the dark side, one of a row of similar houses, but it had a dark secret. The other houses were neat, with tidy, normal people inside. Here it was abnormal, with many signs of anarchy at work. The people who lived here were not ordinary citizens of Mechelen, the old fashioned city of music, metal working, furniture, tapestries and the incredible St Rombout's Cathedral. They were actually plotting to change the map of Europe one day. Each of them had a role to play, but they were of different nationalities and did not know each other well except through their common task. That such a motley group could have taken up residence in the city which hosted the Court of Savoy in the 16th Century, and where the Habsburg-Burgundy dynasty lived and ruled, where the Emperor Charles the fifth was educated, and still hope to remain un-noticed, was a case of hope mis-placed. Their presence in Donkerlei was noted and remarked upon by the neighbours, particularly those next door at Numbers 4 and 8.

The doorbell at Number 6 rang loudly with a sound like a carillon of bells from St Rombout's tower - which it had been designed to imitate, and in doing so irritate the musically minded visitor. A red light glowed over the outside of the brown front door, and then went out. Jan Brouwers looked through the spyhole, after which he opened the door, and in walked Igor Heisenberg.

The two men came from completely different backgrounds. Igor was a Russian, the result of a union between a German officer on the Russian front, who later died during the Soviet advance, and a Ukrainian girl who found herself the mother of a half German, half Russian child. She called him Igor, after the Borodin opera Prince Igor, and gave him his father's surname. He was a shortish, fair haired, muscular man, quiet in manner but noticeably the intellectual of the trio.

Jan was a Mechelen citizen at the time of the German occupation, and had lost his parents when they were rounded up and held at the ancient Austrian army barracks - the Dossin Kaserne - in the early hours of a miserably wet morning in 1941, to be transported by rail to an extermination camp in Germany. The barracks were situated beside a mainline railway track, and so Mechelen became an ideal centre for the deportation of Dutch and Belgian Jews to the concentration camps in Germany and Poland. Although the Brouwers family were accused of being Jewish, in reality their house was needed for the occupation forces, and it was Heisenberg whose family was Jewish - such is the vicious and contrary nature of war. The KGB had recruited both men to act out their fantasies of revenge in the service of a foreign power, Jan out of a genuine desire to avenge his wartime experiences, still vividly in his mind.

"Hello Igor! How did it go in Calais?" Jan greeted Igor with his customary enthusiasm. His dark, debonair features crinkled into a welcoming smile. He was a tall, well built citizen of Mechelen, hardly showing his fifty-five years. They had been good to him, after a very poor start under the Occupation, but he had prospered after the war and built up a successful furniture business which had kept him active and wealthy.

"I had a most interesting coach tour around the terminal, Jan. But it is enormous, and unfortunately the authorities don't tell you much about it - they just give a quick commentary. But it does look as if a coach could get through the security system. A lorry might be more difficult."

"Look, why don't we go down to the café, Igor - the Hoefijzer, the Horseshoe. I sometimes wonder" - Jan lowered his voice - " if this house was bugged after we arrived, to keep a watch on our activities."

The two men walked up to the cafe two blocks away in Donkerlei. Once inside the dark interior, Jan offered Igor a beer.

The plump patron looked on silently. "Jupiler or Primus - or do you prefer the lager? Stella Artois is brewed nearby in Leuven, and is quite famous."

"A Stella would be fine. I will have to get back soon, though, to make a call to Control."

The two men sat down at a nearby table. "Surely they can wait until we have finished. By the way, Igor, you never did show me how to work your machine. What will happen if you fall under a bus?"

"Well, I will show you sometime. It is simple sending out the transmissions, as they are received automatically - nobody has to be listening at the other end. But you have to encode the message first, with a small computer, called a Cyclox. There is an access code first, then it can translate your text and you send it. It is quite easy. At the other end another machine decodes. It works the other way round, with the same program. But if I fall under a bus, the machine will not work for someone else - it has a virus which comes into action until you kill it with another code word."

"Where did the machine come from?"

"I was given it, with some complicated instructions, by an SVR agent in Moscow called Galina Svetlov, before we came here. She will be coming back in a few days time, to see if there are any problems. So you could be right - I have wondered myself if we are being bugged at Number 6. Galina is from the old KGB, and I don't think she needs to come here except to check up on us."

"Well, please make sure I am here when she calls," said Jan - "you never know what might happen to any of us one day. But before you call Control, we must think first and not make any rash promises about taking the Pegasus coach into the tunnel - if that is what they want. I will have to ask Johan Diedericks if he is prepared to let it go over to England, and we must find a good reason. After all, he owns the company."

"Anyway, Jan, I found out that the terminal is designed to accept coaches on the regular shuttle trains with very few security checks of the passengers or their baggage. It is a different matter with the trucks, though. They have to pass through a special check point, which uses X-rays, and if the inspectors are not satisfied they are allowed to blow up the vehicle in a special demolition area surrounded by concrete walls."

"So, you consider we must use a coach, Igor?"

"I have no doubt that the Spetznatz people will tell us what they want to do, after they have been here and heard our reports, and will probably go over every detail. But remember, this operation is Cosmic Secret, and if you tell Diedericks that we want his coach, and he suspects, that will be a problem. The SVR might even ask for us to be removed in order to preserve their secrets. We will have to be careful, Jan."

"Then we had better persuade Anton to ask Diedericks. After all, he is their driver, so they will listen to him. To change the subject, do you know why this place is called the Horseshoe?" Igor shook his head. "I have no idea."

"It is because it used to be a forge, and made horseshoes for the artillery barracks down the road, before it was pulled down. It must have been busy before and after the battle of

15

Waterloo, I should think. That reminds me, I believe Pegasus Travel is arranging a trip to Waterloo very soon. Why don't we go along, and get to know Diedericks better. Then we can suggest a trip through the tunnel, to Dover or perhaps Canterbury. And then we could have a proper look at the security arrangements."

"That is a good idea, Jan. But let's get back now - I don't like to think that the Patron here is listening - he might remember what we say and pass it on to someone else."

They walked back down Donkerlei in the grey dusk, to find a Gendarme in his dark blue uniform standing near the door of Number 6.

After a moment's hesitation they walked quickly on, but when they returned via the embankment of the river Dijle he was still there.

"Can we help you?" asked Jan Brouwers innocently. "Are you looking for anyone?"

"Do you live here?" asked the Gendarme.

"No, we are visitors," volunteered Brouwers. "Do you have a problem?"

"We have instructions to find out if someone is using an illegal radio transmitter on this side of the river, and Donkerlei seems to be in the centre of the area under investigation." The word Donkerlei sent a shiver down Jan's spine.

"That sounds strange. Perhaps it's the stormy weather we've been having. Are you from the headquarters of the Gendarmerie?"

"This is my identity card. I will come back in a few days." With that the Gendarme walked away, leaving them wondering what was going on. Igor was not perturbed.

"Don't worry, Jan, my transmitter sends messages to either Moscow or via East Berlin, if that is required," he said when they were back inside Number 6, "so that should make it much harder to follow. And anyway it is concealed in a special box with a false bottom - I don't think anyone could find it even if they were holding the box in their hands. The contents are heavy, the transmitter underneath is light, so nobody could suspect there is a false bottom."

"Well, if you do have to suspend transmissions, how will you communicate with Control?" asked Jan.

"Galina Svetlov is our link with Control, and will visit us here if transmissions stop, so we must continue. Perhaps we should take the machine to another place to send the signals. I can route the calls through East Berlin using a short aerial if necessary."

"I will think about that," said Jan. He had no wish to make things any more complicated than they were. Just then the doorbell rang with its synthetic carillon chimes. Jan went to look through the spyhole, then opened the door.

"Enter, my friend Anton!"

The visitor was a slightly tubby, balding man in his early sixties. He had spent too long in the driving seat of a touring coach. "Good evening Jan. I am a bit late, but I took the coach on a long trip to Mons - you know, Europe's huge military HQ is there - and also to the Menin Gate at Ypres. You have to wait until the trumpeter has sounded the Last Post and everyone feels satisfied that they have paid their respects to the dead of World War One. That took quite a long time, although it was rather moving, I must admit."

"Are you suggesting that we are getting ready for World War Three, Anton?" Jan's joke fell flat in the company present, even if it was true and they knew it. Their mission might easily lead to another conflict.

"I hope not. But between the three of us and our masters, we might be starting something that could end up that way. Millions of people slaughtered and nothing but ruination to show for it. That I don't ever want to see again."

Jan lowered his voice. "I feel it might be unwise to speak like that in front of Igor - he is a serious Russian, but I, as a

17

Belgian, am only a serious anti-Nazi. And you Polish have always had to sit uncomfortably on both sides of the fence. But the time may come when that won't be enough to stop the forces of chaos. What was it that Jean Cocteau said? Something like: 'History is a combination of accident and luck'. We might push our luck too far if we are careless, but don't tell that to our paymasters, the KGB or SVR as they now pretend to be. In reality nothing has changed in Moscow - not even the food queues."

Anton's wartime history was even more harrowing than either Jan's or Igor's. His family was rounded up in Warsaw after the Polish collapse and the Nazi purge against Jews and dissenters. They were pushed roughly into cattle trucks and sent by rail to Auschwitz-Birkenau, a little Polish army barracks that was turned into the biggest slaughterhouse the world has ever seen. They travelled slowly for five days and nights without food, water or sanitation. On arrival at the remote and densely overcrowded extermination centre, the survivors of the journey were herded and pushed into two groups: one on the left, destined for the gas chamber, the other on the right picked to work until they dropped and died in a living hell.

Young Anton swiftly realised which group was which, and managed to move into the right hand line, urged on by his distraught family, who by now also realised the future that awaited them. They stayed, to avoid drawing attention to Anton's movements, and were duly executed, slowly and painfully, in the choking clouds of insecticide that was Zyklon B gas. After three years of degradation, starvation and disease, the camp was liberated by the Red Army, and the few pathetic survivors were free to go. They had quarried millions of metric tonnes of stone, but otherwise their stay had left no impression at all on the landscape, as if they had never been born.

Most wished over and over again that they had never been

born in the age of the 'final solution', and for Anton it was time to start life again when he finally arrived back in Poland, and saw the utter devastation of his homeland. A young and unemployed drifter, the KGB soon found him, and encouraged his violently anti-German feelings. His arrival at Donkerlei was only one incident in a long series of assignments for his Russian masters. They seemed to get more and more difficult and - in this case - dangerous.

"Anton, you are looking thoughtful," said Jan. "What are Pegasus Travel's plans for next week? I believe you are going to Waterloo."

"Yes, I will be driving the coach. Would you like to come with us?"

"That's an excellent idea. I have a relative who lives at Waterloo. Can you arrange a seat for me? I could help with the commentary if necessary, as I know the story of the battle quite well."

"That should guarantee you a seat, but I don't think it will be necessary. What shall we do with Igor?"

"He may want to come, but one of us will have to stay here so that the station is manned. That's Igor's job as the radio operator, and nobody else knows how to operate his transmitter. So Igor will have to stay and do his job." Jan was in charge of the station, and his word went. Igor reluctantly agreed with Jan. It would have to be another time.

CHAPTER 3

Somewhere Near Moscow

The rain fell incessantly over Moscow that day, a typical October introduction to the freezing spells to come.

A succession of green Volgas, black Chaikas and Zils, and the occasional grey Mercedes took precedence over other traffic along Peace Prospect. At Kolkhoz Square they turned towards the Krestovsky Bridge, past the Cosmos Hotel, and headed on to the Yaroslavl highway which led finally to Kravchenko Village, the home of Forest Lodge, a place completely unknown to the public. The watching pedestrians could not see the back seat occupants of the cars, deep in thought, blinds pulled down in spite of the grey day.

The message had read:

> Your presence is requested at a special meeting of the National Defence Council at Forest Lodge on Wednesday 19th October at 10.00 hours.
>
> Signed in absence   B. Borshkov
> Chairman.

At the mock Scandinavian village hidden among the dripping birch trees, the cars had to negotiate two concentric rows of barbed wire, mined in between and surrouded by watch towers and armed sentries. Dog handlers patrolled in their green uniforms, and sentries checked each Defence Council pass as the bearer was obliged to leave his car and walk to the lodge.

Inside the huge villa, each visitor was escorted to a desk to confirm his name on the admission list, and have his photograph checked. Then he was directed to the elevator, and told to press the Down button to the sixth floor underground - there was no Up button.

On arrival at the sixth floor below, entry to the conference room was again denied until the visitor had again displayed his identity card. Inside the cavernous theatre, backed by an illuminated map of Europe, at least fifty or sixty uniformed generals of the Army and KGB, admirals and Council officials sat expectantly in their serried ranks, waiting for the arrival of the Council Chairman. Soon a portly, grey haired figure dressed in grey uniform with gold trimmed epaulettes entered the theatre and mounted the rostrum, to loud clapping. He held up his hand for a moment.

"Good morning, Comrades. As you know, a special meeting of the Council is only called for exceptional reasons, to discuss military matters of supreme importance to the nation. I trust there has been no disturbance to your busy schedules."

A quiet murmur signified agreement to this unlikely suggestion.

"I will begin, then. Today, we have come to look again at the military situation after the breakdown of the Peace Agreement signed with the Nato countries in Corfu in 1994. You will remember that the German Army was due to conduct joint exercises here in Russia, which they duly did, and we were supposed to go to Germany in 1995 for a major exercise. That agreement broke down because the State of Lower Saxony refused to host the 1995 exercise because of the damage it would cause, and it was cancelled.

"This might not have mattered, had we not received reports that the German exercise in our country was no more than a massive espionage operation, not a genuine step towards mutual cooperation.

"You may say, how do we know about this treachery? The answer can be found in the Codes and Ciphers Department of the General Staff near Arbartskaya Square, where we monitored all the messages to and from the German Army staff in Russia. You will recall that in Brezhnev's work, The Rebirth, he forecast a reconciliation and then a breakdown of trust. It now seems that the old revenge motive of the German military regime has been given new encouragement, after the re-unification of their country in 1989.

"I could counter that by reminding you that, as most of you are aware, there is a gathering revenge motive here in Russia. The difficulties suffered by the German forces in East Germany as the war was ending in our victory were as nothing to the wholesale slaughter inflicted on our citizens by the Nazis in the Great Patriotic War. Our brothers, sisters, mothers, fathers and children who died can never forgive those barbaric actions. None of us can.

"I will now take you through some recent history to set the scene, and then I will ask certain members of Council - who have been forewarned - to comment about the matters we are discussing.

"You may recall that we Russians could have defeated Hitler's war machine on our own, and then taken over control of the whole of Europe. What stopped us, you ask? I will tell you. The Americans and British came into Italy and France at a very late stage, when we had suffered greatly, and managed to roll up the weak Nazi defences in the West, so that they were able to capture Paris, Brussels and a large part of Germany, as well as Italy, before we could fight our way into that part of Europe.

"I can tell you, this would never have been possible without the use of Britain as a safe collection point and base for the Allied invasion forces, which were secure behind the water barrier of the English Channel. Now, what I have to say is strictly Cosmic Secret. With the building of the Channel Tunnel it is still possible for the Americans to reinforce Europe in time of war, but without the tunnel that would be quite impossible. Those vast fleets of landing craft could not be built - or even used - in today's conditions. So, I put it to you, think what the position would be without this new Channel Tunnel, which can move one hundred thousand passengers by train from Britain to Europe every twenty-four hours. Europe would be isolated, at the mercy of the Russian or German armed forces, or both - but this time without any real possibility of external intervention.

"Do you see what I am proposing? Not a repeat of World War Two, of course, but rather a re-run of the pact we had with Adolf Hitler before the Patriotic War, to establish our spheres of influence without any external interference. Then, if my predictions are correct, we could make the running next time, in a much more favourable situation.

"We had not planned initially to have a nuclear war in Europe - because it can all be done by conventional forces - but now we have at our disposal all the nuclear, germ and gas warfare armaments we need to overcome any modern opposition, and there are few American nuclear weapons in the possible theatre of operations. The British have departed, along with most of the G.I.s, and Nato has become an open book since we joined in their planning functions. In my opinion, we have reached a decisive stage in our recent history: to control Europe or not - that is still the question - by peaceful or other means.

"I would like to hear your views now. First, General Zhukov, you had tabled a point of view - may we hear it please?"

A short, heavily built, grey haired general stood up.

"Marshal, my father was involved in Operation Berlin in 1945, as you know, and his forces sustained very heavy casualties during the assault on the city. Initially, he had 750,000 men at his disposal on that one front alone, with 1800 tanks and 3000 aircraft. During the attack on Berlin he suffered 300,000 casualties and lost 2000 tanks, 1200 guns and over 500 aircraft."

"Yes, that is well known, but what is your point of view, General?"

"At that time, Marshal, the enemy consisted of tired and demoralised men, either very young or old, who already knew that they had lost the war. Could we expect this to be the type of resistance we would face if we attempted another drive on Europe?"

"The situation is different in many ways today. A nuclear war is unlikely to start in the early stages, so our conventional forces would dominate again. But they have never been better trained and equipped than they are now, nor do we necessarily intend to fight a war if war can be avoided."

"Do you not consider, Marshal, that another war might take more than six years to complete, unless military production can be increased so as to exceed that of Nato?"

"I do not think we can compare the two situations at all, but thank you for your thoughts and ideas. Now, General Kratsky - you also had something to say on this subject?"

"Yes, thank you, Marshal. As Chief Military Planner I should stress that we do not initially plan to go to war. That outcome would be the last resort of course. Adolf Hitler invented a new style of warfare - the ethnic minority which cries out for help and has to be rescued. World opinion - which does not really exist but has to be invented and stage managed - tends to approve of the idea of rescue, even if it may be declared illegal in the courts of the world. We too have these ethnic minorities, not only in the Baltic states but many others - even in East Germany - and certainly in Poland on a very large scale. These minorities provide us with excuses to intervene, or bargain for territory. The carve-up of Europe could be done by peaceful means to start with, as it was before."

"Exactly, General, I agree. And meanwhile we could be building up our forces for the inevitable Stage Two - which need not concern us today. Admiral Aslov, you were going to give us information about the Channel Tunnel?"

"Yes, Marshal". Another overweight, grey haired identikit man, in the dark blue uniform with gold-trimmed epaulettes of the Russian navy, stood up to speak in a deep and rather tired voice.

"On the wall map here" - he pointed to a diagram of the English Channel presented on the large screen - "we have a plan view and also cross section of the Tunnel. It is about fifty kilometres long and a train takes half an hour to cross. The tunnel's depth below the sea bed varies between 30 and 50 metres, and it would not be possible to destroy the twin rail tunnels or the central service tunnel by conventional explosives in our opinion. The concrete is extremely strong - it is made from Scottish granite, not ordinary concrete - and the chalk based rock surrounding the bores could absorb the shock, as it is elastic.

"To put the tunnel out of action there are several possible methods." Here the admiral brought in a back-projected diagram showing five main alternatives. "Without going into too much detail, you can see that we have looked at five methods for destroying the crossing: surface attack, internal attack by nuclear weapon, flooding by use of the existing British plan to flood the crossing. and two other methods involving either blocking the tunnels or the destruction of one or both terminals. You will be hearing from General Kurbanov of the KGB shortly, and he is involved in research into the security arrangements at the terminals, which are both identical in design. To conclude my point of view, I would find it easier to place a nuclear weapon on the sea bed by submarine, than to use other means. The advantage of this plan is that the weapon can be placed and detonated at any time."

"Admiral, you were going to enlarge on how the British and Americans could manage to reinforce Europe without the tunnel?"

"Ah yes, I was. It must be obvious to any military planner that an invasion fleet of 4700 craft cannot be built today, nor could it sail under a nuclear threat, and so I am sure you agree that if we destroy the tunnel, at the right time - that is before any military alert takes place - we could isolate Europe from the English speaking allies of World War Two."

"General Levin, you also have something to say, I believe?"

"Yes, Marshal. The Russian Air Force could easily destroy the tunnel, by dropping one of our Megaton nuclear weapons on it. The advantages of this method are that no preparation is necessary - our aircraft are always on standby in spite of the recent detente with the West - and we could mount an attack at one or two hours notice. The only problem I foresee, apart from detection of our aircraft, is that we have no exact plan of the tunnel's route, so the placing of a bomb directly over the tunnel is technically not possible at the moment. But we could obtain the necessary information if we need it."

"Thank you, General. I think we should leave that option as a back-up plan for the present, but please make sure we retain that capability."

"Now General Kurbanov, speaking for the Federal Security Service, can you enlighten us about your work to date and your current thinking?"

"Certainly, Marshal. The Defence Council may not be aware that, besides watching an endless stream of sensitive information given out by British and French television channels before, during and after the opening of the crossing in June 1994, we have had a special team on the ground, looking at security arrangements and other details. I will be able to give more information at our next meeting, which I understand will take place next month, but I can confirm that we are in touch with the Irish Republican Army, who have almost completed their study of the Channel Tunnel. They confirm not only their interest in helping us to destroy the crossing, but also that the results of their research into security at the British terminal will be at our disposal - for a price of course. The IRA consider that conventional explosives on the scale of a large car bomb might not destroy the tunnel - that is to say, one tunnel. I should explain that theoretically the tunnel system can operate with only one bore in use, so complete closure might mean that both rail tunnels would have to be destroyed, at the same time preferably."

"And how are you in contact with the IRA?"

"We have occasional radio contact, and the use of dead letter drops also, but our mutual agent in England, romantically code-named The Maid of Kent, is very well informed and is Irish."

"Have you anything else to say at this stage?"

"We have discussed possible ways of destroying the tunnel with our Spetznatz forces, and they believe a small nuclear warhead such as the SS10 rocket can carry would be ideal. We have access to these weapons of course, as we currently guard many of the reserve nuclear stockpiles. The advantage of the nuclear weapon in our opinion is that it renders the area radio-active and so it would be impossible or difficult to repair or use the tunnel after the attack."

"Thank you, General Kurbanov. Before we turn to other matters of interest to the Council, I will give you my summing up so far, and then pose some questions about the future of Europe as it now stands."

A view of Europe appeared on the huge screen. The individual countries were coloured either Red, Pink or Blue.

"In a few months time we will know how the Channel Tunnel can be attacked and eliminated. But here, on this map, we have the layout of Europe by political persuasion." The room went silent, and Marshal Borshkov gestured towards the big screen with a wooden pointer.

"These are the Slav countries in Red. Notice that they include Eastern Europe and the oil producing regions. At present they lack proper direction after the ending of our old union, but they would like the union to return.

"Then we have in Pink the sympathetic states, who won't go to war at any price. For example, in Belgium a recent opinion poll showed that a majority of Belgians would not fight to defend their country. Poland is included as they have not the means to defend themselves, and even Britain is shaded pink for the same reason, as is France. We do not consider their defence plans are viable, as has been demonstrated before.

"Then we have in Blue only one country, obviously Germany, our old adversary. At the centre of Europe and dependant now on alliances which cannot deliver help, we see a country prepared to defend itself up to a point - perhaps not helped by the Communist sympathisers in East Germany - but still totally reliant on help from the United States for survival. That is our opportunity, and that completes my political analysis. Now I will pose three questions which I would like to discuss at our next meeting.

"First of all, are we ready, able and willing to undertake a general strategy of revenge, to recover the honour of our fallen comrades, military or civilian, and their impoverished families? This would be a long term strategy, of course.

"Secondly, can this be done again, as it was intended to be done before the Great Patriotic War, with a non-aggression pact signed with Germany? I am not suggesting a precise timetable now, but please think about it.

"Thirdly, if we need to break our proposed agreements with Germany, how long would it take, and by what means, to secure a Soviet style peace in Europe, which we failed to achieve in 1945? Comrades, until our next meeting, I bid you good-day."

As the audience left the theatre General Zhukov could be heard arguing strongly against the KGB point of view, to the effect that a nuclear war would be unleashed prematurely if a nuclear weapon was used in or on the tunnel.

No-one noticed the Secretary to the Council, Valery Constantin, switching off his tape recorder and picking up his shorthand notes with extreme care. As a loyal Party member he had always managed to keep his influential job, but like many before him he did not really believe in Communist domination as a solution for Europe's future. He had seen the excesses of the apparatchik comrades, with their special pay and privileges, and the abject poverty of the ordinary people, neither of which he shared in. As he went to the elevator Marshal Borchkov stopped him with a hand on his shoulder.

"Valery, don't forget we will need a restricted distribution for the conference minutes today - they are Cosmic Secret and that means an original and one copy only, both delivered to my office this evening. No other copies to be made of course - not even for your own use. Is that understood?"

Constantin smiled blandly. "Naturally, Marshal, it will be done exactly as you say." He always kept copies for his own records anyway, and this was his own secret. Nowadays, the era of the Communist party was over, as far as he was concerned. His loyalty was legendary, but not available at any price.

CHAPTER 4

At MI6 Headquarters in London

It was nearly lunchtime in the opinion of the operators on the 14th Floor of the enormous new Secret Intelligence Service headquarters at Vauxhall Cross, on the south bank of the Thames. It was time to go for sustenance if you were employed on the 13th Floor too, but nobody knew officially that anybody worked there. Like certain American hotels, the 13th floor was omitted because it was considered unlucky. However it did exist, even if no elevators stopped at it. The toilers on eight hour shifts at Floor 13 had to walk there from either the 12th or 14th Floors via a special route masquerading as a fire escape, whose doors were always locked until the would-be entrant had punched in a computerised number - the password for the week.

Allan Gunn on Floor 14 picked up the phone, which was ringing incessantly.

"Hullo, Firearm here."

"We've been trying to fax you. Can you switch on, or is your machine totally kaput?"

"Is that Moonshine?"

"Yeah. Glad you could recognise the voice. We are going to send some news shortly. Stand by, if you will."

"OK, we will await arrival."

Gunn shouted across to his attractive blonde secretary.

"For heaven's sake Sally - isn't your blessed fax working?" Allan could be tactless when he wanted to make an impression.

"Good heavens, it is not," moaned Sally Strang theatrically. "We were just changing the paper - sorry Allan."

"We'll have to send you some paper, but it might be pink" yelled Allan, smiling as he stroked a finger across his throat to indicate a notice of dismissal from the service of the Crown. The fax started to zip out its message:

> Received coded signals from Brussels area by short wave transmission. Code appears to be East German Cyclox. Unable to decrypt owing to code changes. Understand you keep record of Cyclox code shifts and could decrypt on your machine. If so please confirm and we will send what we have.

"Send them an affirmative, Sally." Allan Gunn scribbled a note for her, then he began to feel his hunger pangs subsiding as an idea welled up that there might be something worth following up here. The secret Moonshine listening station in west Germany normally fed Nato HQ at Brussels and either National Security Agency at Ford Meade, Maryland or GCHQ at Cheltenham in England, but if GCHQ did not need to know MI6 was automatically fed, as a backstop.

Allan Gunn, Deputy Director of the West European section of MI6 was an energetic, live wire of a man, who lived on his nerves more often than not. Short, tough, his fair hair starting to recede, he would not stand out in a crowd, but his rapid eye movements betrayed formidable thinking skills. Everyone else on Floor 14 may have been doing his or her job studiously and perhaps meticulously, but Allan had fingers in many pies and liked to trouble-shoot on a loose rein. A bachelor, he had not joined the SIS for a desk job and a steady salary, but for its possibilities of intrigue and uncertainty, which called for intuitive deduction and lateral thinking. He it was who had helped to round up the Klaus Mankovitz team, which had operated freely in Oxfordshire near the Atomic

Energy Authority facility, and passed atomic secrets to a wide range of clients in Europe and the Middle East in exchange for mega-money. The arrest and detention of this sophisticated spy outfit propelled Gunn to his present post of key executive without a fixed portfolio. His job description was vague but contained many references to the word Coordination. The message went down the fax to Germany in clear:

> OK, we will try to read on our equipment, but don't expect anything for an hour or two. Speak to you after lunch.

Allan could see visions of curried lamb cooked in white wine with garlic sauce, followed by strawberries in kirsch, and a good brandy or two afterwards. He spoke again to his faithful secretary of three years standing.

"Sally, could you drive us down to the Tramonti restaurant? I think you deserve a decent meal instead of those curled up sandwiches you seem to keep from one week to the next. We'll leave the car in Hyde Park underground, then you can drive me back when the brandy has disappeared."

After a pleasant meal, at which Allan was, as always, full of admiration for his cool and calm secretary, they walked rather unsteadily back down Hyde Park, crossed the grass to the car park, and descended underground. There a policeman was standing close to the car. He spoke to Allan, somewhat unhelpfully in the circumstances..

"I suppose you are not driving, sir, are you?" Gunn thought of the third brandy and replied with obvious over-emphasis, his voice betraying a state of unnecessary happiness, or so the officer had decided.

"Certainly not, officer, my secretary here is driving today." Allan flashed a look of quiet desperation at Sally.

Sally climbed with some reluctance into the car, backed it

out between the pillars, and urged it slowly up the ramp to the slip road.

"Mr Gunn" - she liked to use his surname when the going became serious - "I really don't think I can drive straight. Wouldn't you like to try? You're usually fairly OK after a few, aren't you?" In truth she was tired out. Life on Floor 14 was not conducive to cheerfulness in the middle of the day. A long afternoon and evening lay ahead for her. Allan was a workaholic, and didn't like to go home early: if only Sally would see why, and give him some magical reason to stop, he might have been able to change his ways.

"Of course, no problem Sally, I quite understand," he muttered thickly, before moving round to the right hand side of the car and driving erratically to the office. At the 13th Floor, which he called into briefly, there was a mass of foreign operators - seemingly from all parts of the globe - beavering away at their paperwork.

"Good afternoon Allan," called the Supervisor of WW13 (Worldwide, 13th Floor).

"How goes it, James?"

James Meredith, a survivor from the many and sometimes untidy military campaigns in which British forces had taken part since the 1939-45 war - undercover in his case - answered cheerily: "Fine, as usual, thanks. In fact a bit too quiet at the moment."

"Well, I may have some news for you. We've just had an intercept from the Nato listening station. Seems to have come from the Brussels area in Cyclox code. Have you seen anything on this?"

"Not as yet, but we do get decrypts from GCHQ of all coded messages from the Nato station, so I can watch out for that and let you know if I find anything."

"OK. I'll be upstairs. Cheerio now."

Allan found his way through the fire escape to the 14th Floor, where his rather solid and rotund Assistant, Ken

Johnson, was waiting for him.

"GCHQ have come up with a decrypt. It seems to be a message to a control station in Russia, which acknowledged it. Here we are." He placed the message on the table.

> Have visited target area and checked security which is extremely high. Suggest we should meet to discuss. A safe area is the open air museum at Middelheim near Antwerp. May I recommend midday 17th this month at the ticket office.

"We seem to have found a new set of cold war warriors here," said Gunn disapprovingly, "or international terrorists. We'll have to follow up, I suppose, with someone from Floor 13. Would you send a message to Moonshine, please. Something like - "Thanks for your message, which we can read. Please send us anything more which seems to come from that source, and we will follow it up".

At the elegant listening station in northwest Germany a forest of aerials and satellite dishes turned and dipped above the tortuous cliff walls towering over the sparkling river below. In the pristine white building complex above, housing an almost wholly American management team and their state-of-the-art equipment, Chuck Waters saw the incoming message.

"OK let's have a look, John. See what's on the tapes and give me a report, please." A 'report' for Chuck usually meant something positive was required within thirty minutes.

Chuck was an old friend of Allan's. They met at the CIA HQ at Langley, Virginia during Allan's short exchange visit. Several bourbons down the road they seemed to have similar ideas and reactions, so the US-UK special relationship really worked in their case, and paid off handsomely during the forthcoming mission.

"Send a message back to SIS please, John." The message read:

> Nice to hear you are making steam, Allan. Will revert
> shortly about your new friends in Belgium. They are
> a lot nearer to me than you actually, but I will leave
> you to handle this one. Coming to London very soon,
> and will expect full treatment. Hang in there. Chuck.

Chuck gave out a chuckle. "He knows what that means. If there's one security service dedicated to way-out entertainment, it's the British. Kinky restaurants, dive bars, weird encounters with Members of Parliament - they have it all in London." After first meeting Allan at CIA, Chuck had gone on to NSA at Fort Meade to study interception and decrypt techniques and to specialise. The NSA and GCHQ in England had an exchange agreement which ensured a regular flow of high grade intelligence in both directions. Chuck's next career step, closer to the real action which he and Allan craved, was to the Nato listening station. Here he was at the cutting edge of intercept techniques, which were to complement Allan's undoubtedly fine investigative talents. Back in England, Allan's fax whizzed again:

> We have no other messages on tape but will watch
> that frequency and report. Seems your Belgian
> friends have only just started up their broadcasting
> activities. Best of luck and be assured we will give it
> our best shot. Chuck.

The scrambler phone rang again and Allan picked it up.

"Tim Hutchins from Whitehall. The opposition. Is that Allan?"

"It certainly is. What moves in Five?"

"We've got this signals intercept from Belgium via HQ and it seems to be a terrorist outfit over there. We wonder if you've heard of it?"

"Just got the same message. We are going to follow up by

dropping in on the meeting - without saying hello to these folks of course."

"That sounds good, Allan. No doubt you'll keep us informed, as usual?"

"We certainly will. Goes without saying, Tim."

"Thanks, Allan. I am sure you remember when we were rather upset in 1994 by our friends in the Emerald Isle, who decided to bring an enormous bomb through Heysham port. It came from County Down, as you probably know. I wish those idiots would stick to Irish laments, instead of all this Guy Fawkes stuff. The next thing was a call from the Minister, who wanted a review of security in the Channel Tunnel - not surprising, I suppose."

"Yes, I gather we've finally armed the British bobby on the beat at the French terminal."

"Correct. The French police operating over here - the *Police de l'Air et des Frontières* - are sensibly armed to the teeth with Heckler & Koch rapid firing machinery, so now we've followed suit. Anyway, we have passed that signal decrypt to the French DST, who will obviously inform their terminal at Calais. I wonder if you would like to come to the Minister's next security briefing?"

"Yes, I think that would be useful - I assume these blokes carrying their smoking bombs operate on both sides of the water?"

"Could well be. Thinking of that intercept, when they talked of very high security, could that be Calais in your valued opinion?"

"Why not," said Allan reflectively. "We should find out something when we drop in on these bandits at Middelheim, but maybe we won't succeed entirely. I trust you will keep an ear open for any more signals from that neck of the woods, via HQ of course, in case we miss something."

"Certainly, we'll keep you in the picture Allan, you can be sure," said Hutchins, putting the phone down.

Allan turned to his Assistant, Ken Johnson, who was hovering.

"Ken, if you were trying to blow up the Channel Tunnel, which is controlled from Folkestone until control passes to Calais in an emergency, which end would you plan to attack?"

"I presume it would be the French end. Granted, the IRA planned an attack from this side, but that was a failure. They don't repeat their failures, apparently. They like to surprise all the time."

"Right, so that is why you think the next attack would be planned in France?"

"Yes, I should think the Russians would be the first choice, followed by the East German communists who want to return to the status quo ante - they must be the only ones interested in getting rid of the tunnel permanently. They might do the planning anywhere in Europe, but my guess would be France or Belgium, which have direct rail links with the tunnel, then Holland or Germany. The closer they are to the target, the more information they can get about local conditions, such as security."

"That's it, Ken!" Allan hit upon the word security. "Maybe that's why we heard that message about tight security. You seem to be well on your way to a second career in fortune telling, if your theory is correct. Who was it who said: 'It may be all right in practice, but does it work in theory?' He may have had a point there."

"Would you like me to brief someone on Floor 13 for a quick trip to the capital of Europe - via the tunnel of course?" suggested Johnson, rather too carelessly, as he was just about to find out.

"I think we will have to plan this attack carefully. The open air museum at Middelheim is a large park full of valuable statues - including two of our own Henry Moore's major works - according to the Belgian guide books. So when these people arrive at the ticket office - as they will have to - we must try to recognise them and then follow them. We need two people who speak Flemish, French and probably Russian too, dressed as tourists and equipped with all the photographic and listening gear they can carry. See what Floor 13 has available for that week, so that we can reconnoitre the place and get to know the park better than the terrorists, before they arrive. I don't think we should try to snatch one, because that could kill the operation, so it can be a peaceful mission, but it could get tricky. Better have the two people armed with something useful in case."

"OK Allan, I will check that out and let you know by the end of the day." Ken Johnson had been a slim, weasel faced man who had survived several scrapes in Eastern Europe, but had put on weight as the paperwork in MI6 increased. He used to be thin enough to hide behind a pillar if necessary, but those days, he hoped, were definitely over now. His pension was only a few years away, and his receding hair, seen all too frequently in the bathroom mirror, made him thoughtful and at times distinctly miserable. However his finest hour was yet to come.

"One other thing, Ken, I may have to send you along on this mission. I doubt if two is enough. Be prepared to take charge, will you? You'll enjoy a little holiday in the heart of Europe, don't you think?"

The suggestion went crashing down like a lead weight, nearly causing Ken to have a premature thrombosis, but he managed to preserve a calm balance. After all, his Annual Assessment was due to be drafted any day.

"I suppose it might be quite a change from Floor 14," he replied without a great deal of conviction - and perhaps too defensively for his own good. After all, those who did not enjoy the occasional foray into the outer jungle were of little value to MI6, and he knew it.

"I'm sure you will enjoy every minute of the art lessons they provide in Belgium - and of course they are all free," joked Allan, sensing Ken's evident unease at the vague nature of the proposed mission. "And you never know where it may lead."

"A knighthood perhaps?" Ken's joke played on the unreality the two men often shared in their chosen career, which was beginning to pall for him at that moment.

CHAPTER 5

In the Moscow Area

The sunlight slanted through the grey spruce trees around the closely guarded dacha as Boris Borchkov stood to address his faithful Military Council - all hurriedly summoned without aides, to an extraordinary planning conference. Numbers were restricted, as was the subject matter.

The room was lit only by a dull evening glow as the hushed audience waited to hear the purpose of the meeting. This was the type of historic meeting which the West had never seen on its television screens.

"You have been asked to come here today to discuss the future not only of our great historic country but perhaps of the world itself." His voice was heavy and his accents measured in tone and gravity. "An event of tremendous importance to our strategic thinking has occurred. I refer to the construction of the Channel Tunnel linking Britain with France. From now on we have to compress our strategic planning into months rather than years or decades." Marshal Borchkov paused for his introduction to sink in. The audience was silent.

"It is popularly supposed that this tunnel could be severed by nuclear weapons. But this may never be the case. A nuclear war is now unthinkable. The Cold War is over, the stakes are too high. In any case the governments of the USA, Britain and France have already decided to spend an enormous amount of money on defending the tunnel and their entente cordiale. This expenditure is not needed just to maintain the link between the two countries, but to ensure that it will remain in place indefinitely, as part of their strategic planning. Why, you may ask, should they do this if a nuclear war is unthinkable?" Borchkov's voice fell almost to a conspiratorial whisper.

"Because this tunnel will ensure that Europe can always be reinforced by the United States via its bases in Britain. I can tell you that the USA has already earmarked one hundred thousand men to be flown to Britain at a few days notice if there is a threat of general war, and they will have over-riding powers to act anywhere in western Europe as the Americans decide. Until now it was impossible to move American troops into Europe without total air superiority - air supremacy in fact - which we could always have at any time and place of our choosing, in the event of another war in Europe, using our latest high speed, high performance aircraft which we have never shown to the West.

"Now, another review of recent history, so that we are all thinking along the same track. The key to world domination remains Europe. At present there are three effective power blocs in the world, omitting China which continues to slumber and may one day have serious internal problems, and Japan which only has local and trade interests in Asia and the Pacific area: they are Russia, the USA and Europe. The USA gained its position in the last half of this century largely by means of the Great Patriotic War during which she prospered by late intervention, while the other major participants were mortally wounded as great powers and lost their influence owing to the very serious damage suffered by their economies. Our plans, as you are now well aware, are aimed at supremacy in the 21st Century, when we shall become the guiding hand and controller of Europe's and perhaps the world's future, helped in those aims by the two other power blocs - though not at their own choice.

"America will always settle for a separate peace to avoid another major conflict. Then two worlds will co-exist, the old and the new.

"China may become a super-power in the coming century, but is still too backward to act globally. So a race has now started - which we must and will win - to ensure that there are only two super-powers: Russia with Europe incorporated, and the USA and its allies, including Britain. China will then be under our indirect control, not idealogically but because it shares the same land mass.

"The American hold on Europe originates in the 17th Century when English, Scottish and Irish settlers arrived to colonise it, followed by others from Germany and the rest of Europe. A common language developed - American English - and cooperation in two major wars has ensured that the USA and Europe became united militarily. However the two have become separated since the Great Patriotic War, and we could arrange for that to work to our advantage. The Nato defence system requires that nuclear weapons are not used during the first few weeks of general war, and that time would be used to reorganise the European armies and air forces. Nevertheless if nuclear weapons were not used, for one reason or another, whether by a wish to avoid casualties or to avoid throwing the first fatal stone - then the defence of Europe will fail. However if nuclear weapons are threatened or actually used, we can always retaliate by blocking the channel tunnel, so the builders and operators of that subway to Europe would need to make it nuclear-proof. But that is not possible, according to our studies of the technology of the tunnel.

"Now we turn to more modern history. How many allies in Europe does the United States have? At our last conference we looked at the red, the pink and the blue areas of Europe and its hinterland. The red represented our former empire, most important of which are still our allies. The pink represented those which would not fight, and only blue Germany would be faced with the classic decision according to Shakespeare: to be, or not to be - we could substitute the word 'fight' for 'be' without altering the eventual meaning. If we were to guarantee Germany's present frontiers by a non-aggression treaty such as Molotov signed in August 1939, there would be room for both of us to manœuvre, but very little room for others to do so.

"At our last conference at Forest Lodge, I asked you to think about the future: to think whether we wish to avenge the many millions of our fallen comrades and citizens - which the public now demands more and more all the time - and whether by a non-aggression treaty we could proceed to control Europe. With that introduction I will now ask various speakers to give their opinions."

The room erupted in sustained clapping, which continued for several heady but ominous minutes. The rest of the meeting continued in camera, and apparently no records exist.

In another part of Moscow later that week, at a KGB conference centre near the old Rossiya Hotel, General Kurbanov held his own briefing, with an audience of over 40 officers and senior operators of the KGB and SVR - the new state security service. The room had been swept for bugs before the meeting as usual: only a few weeks earlier a listening device the size of a small coin was found stuck to the outside corner of a window frame, but as no markings were found it was impossible to discover which of the world's intelligence services was listening. The main KGB offices at Lubyanka, it was decided, would not be used for this conference because bugging there - by opponents of the current Russian government - had become a serious menace to those who transacted official business: the number of leaks had multiplied and the security of the state was frequently put at risk. Microphones the size of pin-heads were now being used by all the major intelligence services, and there was a strong feeling in the KGB that the coin-sized receptors were being planted to distract attention from the presence of more modern devices.

The burly figure of General Kurbanov thrust its way to the stage and walked to the dais. The audience was hushed, as was appropriate at a KGB presentation. All ears strained to hear what was to come.

"I apologise for the parking facilities here - we have far too many private cars now in our country. We will be able to recall your drivers from the KGB car park at the end of the meeting, and while they are returning to collect you we will have time to test the Stolichnaya and caviar, which I understand our loyal staff will be providing as a reward for your efforts here today." A buzz of excitement fed on itself for a few moments, before subsiding as the audience realised the gravity of the matters under discussion.

"Now we have come here to take our planning for the channel tunnel - Operation Kingdom - a stage further. At some time in the next few months we must be ready, if asked by the Supreme Council, to put the tunnel out of action. The decision as to exactly when, will of course be taken at some future date and we will be the last to be informed." This joke went down well amongst the cynics of the KGB present - which included almost the entire audience.

"I should explain that the British - our old allies in the past and by no means slow to think of a good idea - have already built into the tunnel two systems of destruction on their side of the waterway. They can either flood the tunnel - which would not necessarily be a permanent state of affairs, or they can destroy the rail tracks and supports, which are carried on special piers at a low point in the tunnel. Either way, it would be put out of action completely, although using the second method only, the track could be repaired. All this information came from our informer who penetrated Transmanche-Link, the tunnel builders, at an early stage. As a result we have full details of how the tunnel can be flooded. There is a large water main running into the tunnel which carries water for fire fighting, and this can be opened up at the lowest point, just over half way between Calais and Folkestone. As yet, we believe nobody has made a plan to drain the tunnel after flooding. Now, I will ask my Deputy, General Suslev, to describe the ways in which we propose to disable the tunnel, on the assumption that we will not be able to flood it - maybe this is not a wise assumption, but that is the present view here in the KGB."

"Good morning, comrades," said Suslev. "You are aware that we have proposed five methods to disable the channel tunnel, apart from attacking it from the air with a nuclear weapon, a step we consider might escalate out of our control. The methods are shown on the display, in reverse order of priority." The screen lit up.

OPERATION KINGDOM - THE CHANNEL TUNNEL
Methods of Attack

1. *Conventional explosives.* These would be so large that they would be detected, as the Irish Republican Army discovered in July 1994.

2. A *Nuclear Weapon* delivered by:
   Submarine. This has the advantage that the mission can be set up at any time, and be activated later, but it is almost impossible to position the weapon exactly over the tunnel.

   A Freight Wagon attached to a freight train. This poses some difficulties in connecting to the train, and could be detected very easily, as the freight documents would be used to check out the load.

   A Tourist Coach, or Car, driven into the tunnel from the Calais terminal. The security system is less strict for tourist vehicles than for heavy lorries. We consider a car is too easy to inspect and so a coach would be better.

A Heavy Goods Vehicle driven into the tunnel. Like cars and coaches, this would travel on a shuttle train, but would be subject to special and much more strict search techniques - even X-rays according to our agents based in Belgium.

END

The screen went blank, and General Suslev continued his set piece speech.

"We consider, at the moment, that either of the last two methods of placing a nuclear warhead" - here Suslev illuminated the screen again for a few moments - "would be most likely to succeed. The warhead can come from stocks retrieved from East Germany, which have disappeared from their bunkers and are now almost untraceable. We would of course try to make it look as if the East German comrades had perpetrated the foolhardy act of war - so I insist that these words are not repeated outside this room. If there were to be a leak, we would naturally ask all of you to take lie detector tests, and we all know how painful the KGB lie detector tests are supposed to be.

"In order to verify all the details before we make a final decision, we are sending a Spetznatz team to Belgium to meet our existing group there, and they will bring back enough information, on this or another visit if necessary, to enable us to finalise more detailed plans. These obviously might range from breaking into the tunnel with a Spetznatz team or simply sending the explosives in by other means. Nothing has been decided yet. Now, can I have any comments please?"

At that moment, the fire alarm sounded and the building had to be evacuated into the street outside. There is no record of the second part of the meeting, as the Secretary was suddenly taken ill and no minutes were kept after the alarm sounded. As it was, the minutes for the first part of the conference had to be recovered from the Secretary at a hospital waiting room, thus placing him under the greatest suspicion until it was realised that his brief case was still securely locked, albeit by a coded number unknown to anyone else. This still led to his suspension from duty, and a process of virtual interrogation to see if a copy had been made during his absence. Eventually his unexplained absence was found to be due to 'Afghan syndrome', a serious psychological condition known to Russian medical science, due to the unfortunate man's detention for several months in an Afghan rebels' prison camp, where the conditions were almost as barbaric as the Lubyanka prison, and the prisoners were summoned to interrogation by an alarm call which sounded exactly like the fire alarm at the conference centre that day.

As it happened, the reality was different. The secretary was a CIA mole, and he had availed himself of the KGB equipment, purchased from the USA, to download his laptop computer while waiting for the priority treatment which he did not need on this occasion. The resulting mini-disk recording the salient points of the meeting was duly despatched to an agent able to contact the American intelligence network, but the information it contained was regarded as either too bizarre to be true, or a deliberate plant, so no further action was taken except to file it. The East-West detente marched on, in spite of the warning signs.

CHAPTER 6

Near Waterloo

At Mechelen it was another dull day in Donkerlei, the dark lane. The three conspirators at Number 6 were up early, Victor upstairs with his transmitter and the other two downstairs preparing for an early start on their trip to Waterloo. Igor came down looking serious.

"I have a message from Control confirming that they will meet us at Middelheim on the 17th as we suggested. You know the place don't you, Anton?"

"Yes, that is one of the Pegasus Travel destinations. We call it the Statue Park because the park is full of original statues. Where did you arrange to meet up? The park covers a huge area."

"I told them to meet us at the ticket office at midday. Then we will have to find a quiet place to talk - what do you suggest, Anton?"

"When I last went there, the restaurant was crowded and did not have enough separation - you can be overheard from the next table too easily. But there is another part of the display across the road which is more private, and we could direct them to meet us at one of the big exhibits - I remember seeing a large brick building without any windows, which is easy to recognise. Also, not far from the ticket office there is a moat round the old house, which is surrounded by trees, and we could start our meeting there."

"I suppose our transmissions to Moscow cannot be intercepted, can they?" asked Jan, the team leader.

"No. The code is computerised and it automatically changes as the time moves on. That's why it is called a Cyclox. The clock inside the encoder keeps moving on."

"You mean it shifts all the time?"

"Yes. You punch in the date and time, then send the message to Control. Their machine is set to the same time, within fifteen minutes, so they can read the coded message."

"OK, but suppose someone else has the same machine as yours, can't they decode the message?" asked Jan.

"Not unless they have the access code," replied Igor. "That has to be dialled in first, and it changes every week."

"But now that we have attracted the local Gendarmes' attention, surely we ought to stop sending messages? One more visit from them and we could be in trouble," said Jan.

"Yes, I think so. That is why I asked them to come here and discuss the situation. We may have to use the phone, but that is even more risky - our line might be tapped for all we know - unless we use the old KGB telephone code."

"Let us discuss that when they come on the 17th," said Jan. "Now, where do I pick up the Pegasus coach today, Anton? You said it stops in the Wool Market, and by Saint Rombout's Tower. Also you mentioned the Kyrenia floating restaurant on the river Dijle."

"Whichever you prefer. I will keep you a seat, and you can recognise the coach by its flying horse markings on the back and sides. We will leave the Wool Market at ten, so that would be the easiest to remember. I will wait for you there. Then we arrive at Waterloo by eleven."

"What are we going to see there, Anton?" said Jan.

"First we have a snack at the Bivouac de l'Empereur, which is named after Napoleon, then we climb up the Victory Monument which was built by the Allies, and overlooks the battlefield. There will be a short description of the battle, then we go down to the Museum and the cinema for a modern film of the battle. Finally we go into the Panorama building, which has a big circular display in three dimensions. As you have been there before, you could visit your relative when we come down from the monument, if you want to. We will spend more than an hour in the cinema and panorama."

"Right, Anton, I will see you at the Wollemarkt at ten - make sure you don't go without me!"

When the coach arrived at the site of the battle, Anton parked opposite the Bivouac de l'Empereur. The old-fashioned inn was built shortly after the battle, using souvenirs of the conflict to decorate its dark corners and walls. Jan sat with Anton at a small table behind the inn to enjoy the bright morning sunshine.

"When do we climb the Monument, Anton?"

"That will be shortly after midday. I hope you are feeling strong - the steps are very steep, but there is a handrail to hang on to."

"Don't worry about that. Tell me, how was the monument created?"

"The guide will tell you all about it. The mound was built by hand, with soil collected in baskets, mainly by the women of Waterloo."

The climb to the top of the monument lived up to its reputation as the coach party strained to reach the summit, hanging tightly onto the rail. A great vista of the historic battlefield stretched out in front. The guide, a plump dark-complexioned man who might have been one of Napoleon's more elderly warriors himself, addressed his audience without waiting for them to recover their breath.

"Did you enjoy the climb?" A silence gave him the answer, and he continued.

"Does anyone here know the story of the battle?" Another silence, so the guide pressed on with his well rehearsed speech.

"Ladies and gentlemen, welcome to the Victory Monument, which was erected after the historic battle of

Waterloo. Very few people know that in 1812 Napoleon had only just escaped from the island of Elba, where he had been imprisoned by the English. But his enormous influence and personal magnetism were such that he was able to gather together most of his old generals and an army of over seventy thousand men, with their muskets, artillery pieces and horses, in only three months. Then he advanced from Paris to Brussels, and it seemed that nothing could stop him from taking the city. The Duke of Wellington had to move very quickly to defend Brussels with his smaller army, which was out-numbered by about ten thousand - a dangerous state of affairs when the opponent was Napoleon.

"A Prussian army under Marshal Blucher was resting nearby, after a skirmish with Napoleon's advance guard, and might be relied on to fight if the Marshal could be persuaded, but it was not ready to move, and nobody knew where and when the battle would be fought. It was Napoleon's favourite trick, when opposed by two separate forces, to attack them in turn so that he could outnumber his opponents one at a time before they could combine forces for the battle.

"Now, we are standing on a mound of earth over forty metres high and nearly one hundred and seventy metres wide at the base. As you are all aware, it has one hundred and twenty-eight steps. It was built by the Dutch, who fought on the English side, with help from the citizens of Waterloo. I am afraid it was mainly the ladies who did the work - as always - and they carried thirty-two thousand cubic metres of soil up this slope in hand baskets. The bronze lion statue on top was cast in Mechelen - of course Belgian soldiers also fought on the English side. The lion weighs twenty-eight tonnes, and had to be transported by steamship most of the way, then on a huge chariot pulled by twenty horses. It stands on a masonry plinth four and a half metres high - can anyone suggest how the lion was lifted forty-five metres up to its present position?"

A voice volunteered: "It must have been lifted on a special trolley, I suppose, by horses pulling on ropes?"

"You are quite right, M'sieur," the guide replied with a brief smile of satisfaction. "I think you must have been here before. Now the Duke of Wellington managed to find out where Napoleon intended to fight the battle, at the last moment. So he went to the famous ball in Brussels on the eve of the battle, to give the impression that he was not ready, but he moved his army into position here at Waterloo in the two days before and after the ball. Napoleon had already defeated part of the Prussian army at Ligny, on his way to Quatre Bras where he intended to fight, so he felt confident of another French victory."

The guide paused for effect. He was pleased with his dissertation, and pressed on with renewed vigour to the main story.

"The Duke had one important advantage, you must understand - he had arrived first on the battlefield. He was able to fortify three groups of buildings which you can see to the left, to your front, and at the right hand side - Papelotte farm, the castle of Hougoumont, and La Haie Sainte farm. Also Napoleon's men were exhausted by their long march in cold and wet weather, and by their earlier battle with the Prussians, so he waited until the 18th of June to start the battle. Then he launched six regiments into an assault on Hougoument castle, the English centre, but the defenders managed to hold on with enormous losses. The building caught fire and finally collapsed under the weight of the French artillery bombardment, so yet more casualties were suffered by the heroic defenders.

"So then Marshal Ney, Napoleon's favourite commander, who had turned the tide of battle many times before, was sent in to attack La Haie Sainte, to your right over there" - the guide pointed dramatically - "but did not succeed, and the Emperor's legendary Guard regiments had to be sent in to finish off the defenders. They were winning and a French victory seemed inevitable, when Marshal Blucher's sixty thousand Prussians arrived on the bloody scene from the woods far over to your left. Those woods have long since disappeared, and so has the hill which prevented Napoleon from seeing, with his telescope, Blucher's sudden advance. That hill was levelled after the battle, and much of it was transported here to build this monument, so you will have to imagine it hiding the Prussian advance from Napoleon's ever watchful eye.

"At that moment Napoleon's victory disappeared with the shouts of the charging Prussian cavalry, and of Wellington's own three regiments of Hussars, which went in to attack the French strong points of Quatre Bras and La Belle Alliance farm. The French Guard regiments were outnumbered, but they bravely formed squares to cover Napoleon's retreat, and held out to the last man. The carnage was dreadful and the Emperor had lost his next crown. That night Papelotte farm was relieved, and Wellington met Blucher at La Belle Alliance just as it was getting dark. Napoleon fled the battle in his special coach but was tracked down by the Prussian cavalry, and had to gallop away on horseback. He reached Charleroi at five next morning, where he was recognised and captured.

"And so it happened that the Napoleonic era, which had taken the Emperor all the way to Austria, Italy, Germany, Spain and Russia, ended with a last journey to Saint Helena in the Atlantic, where he spent six years dictating his memoirs until he died at the early age of fifty-two. The story has it that he was poisoned by the staff at his home on the island, but that has never been proved. Anyway, Napoleon's death did not stop his legendary hold on French minds, and his body was brought back to Paris and carried in state through the Arc de Triomphe to be buried at Les Invalides. For a general who had lost more than two million soldiers in battle it was a tremendous honour, bestowed upon possibly the most powerful man who had ever lived until that time."

The guide stopped to draw breath. It had been a stirring performance as always. He never felt unmoved by his own tale of the epic battle. "Now, would anyone like to ask a question?"

Jan found himself unable to resist the invitation.

"Do you not find it strange that in 1812, public enemy number one was France, then in 1914 and 1939 it was Germany, then Russia in 1945? How do you think this can be explained - I mean the constant change of aggressor and victim?"

"That, my friend, is the tragedy of mankind, with his readiness to fight for territory and the spoils of war, and the part which dictators play in all this. I can only say that change is constant, and I think the drama will go on, even if we cannot understand why."

"You mean, we could have another European tragedy?" Jan asked the question to draw out his knowledgable guide's thoughts still further. The guide avoided the question.

"Wait until you see the Panorama of the battlefield later, M'sieur. You will see tragedy enough for one day," he replied morbidly. "Do we have any other questions?"

"Can you say how many casualties were suffered in the battle?"

"The records showed that a quarter of all the men taking part in the battle were killed here, and many others were wounded."

"Is it true that the Germans used this monument as an anti-aircraft gun position during the war?"

"That is quite true. So the country which came to the rescue of an English general during the 19th Century ended up fighting against England in the 20th. I can quite understand if you feel that history takes very unusual turns, as our first questioner suggested."

"Is it not a fact that Marshal Blucher had to be persuaded to fight at Waterloo, and would have preferred not to?"

"Yes, that is quite right. As I said before, the Marshal wanted to rest his troops and horses. Luckily for us Belgians, the Duke of Wellington managed to make him change his mind, and the history of Europe was completely altered."

The guide's last remark was not lost on Jan Brouwers. He never felt totally committed to the dangerous plan being devised by the SVR. After stepping slowly down to the base of the monument he went across the road to the Bivouac de l'Empereur and caught a taxi to his sister's house at 19, Avenue Floreal near the town of Waterloo. He directed the driver towards the old golf course, now converted into a large estate of beautiful white houses with flower-filled gardens. Marie Brouwers came to the door, looking excited after Jan's phone call from the Bivouac.

"Such a nice surprise to see you, Jan - what brings you here. Can you stay and have a chat? I want to know what you are up to these days. Is all well with you?" Marie was a charming lady, and devoted to her tall, dark and handsome brother, although they met infrequently nowadays.

"I am still at Mechelen of course, retired from the furniture business. I take in lodgers - two at the moment - to keep me in funds. I came here because one of my guests drives a travel coach for Johan Diedericks - do you remember him? - and of course to see you."

"What does your other lodger do?" enquired Marie innocently.

Jan paused, then said matter-of-factly: "He is doing a study of town planning for a Russian firm. He's half German and half Russian. He doesn't say much about it, except that Mechelen is a beautiful place to study." Jan found himself telling lies too easily, and regretted the need to mislead his sister. He might need her help one day, if things got difficult, then he would have to reveal much more.

"And how are you managing to live these days, Marie?"

"Much the same. It has been a fine summer for the garden, but the weather is so cold now. I am still doing some part-time work in the museum here in Waterloo. The tourists seem to come in greater numbers every year. What did you think of the new display and the film of the battle?"

"I didn't stay for that, but the guide at the Victory monument was very good, and I remembered again that we and the Boche fought the French then, but this century has been quite different. I wonder what will happen next."

"I think you can rest assured that with our new European allies and Nato looking after us, all will be well next time - there won't be a next time, I mean."

"I hope you are right," Jan said, thinking of the dangerous mission he had undertaken. He stopped at that, and with a few remarks about the fine state of the garden he decided to leave. The others must be waiting for him by now.

"I will get you our local taxi to take you back," said Marie, and it duly came to the gate.

Jan arrived in time to meet the party coming out of the Panorama building, but was curious to have another look inside. He climbed upstairs to the platform at the centre of the circular display. Nothing had changed since his last visit, but the impression was even more intense. The hundred metre wide pastiche of exhausted soldiers and horses, most in a state of lingering death, and the impression of destruction on a smoke-ridden and deafening battlefield, made him more certain now that he would have nothing to do with war in future. When he went down to the coach he found Anton was also subdued. They climbed aboard the coach, Anton in the driver's seat, Jan behind him. There was time for reflection.

"What did you think of the Panorama, Jan?" asked Anton.

"I didn't feel like starting another war, if that's what you mean. What did you think of it?"

"I have seen it several times, but let's hope it never

happens again in our time, eh?"

A subtle change had come over both men. The passage of nearly two centuries had not altered the brutal message. They drove off in silence, deep in their private thoughts.

Arriving back at Donkerlei they found Igor in a state of alarm.

"Jan, that unfriendly gendarme came here today. He talked about radio transmissions again. I told him we know nothing about it, but he was welcome to come inside. He refused, so I suppose all is well, but we must stop our transmissions now. I will have to set up another way of contacting Control. If we are found out, you know what will happen to us?"

"Yes," said Anton quietly. "They will first disown us, and then try to eliminate us."

"I am sure you did the right thing, Igor," said Jan coolly. "We will send no more messages, but you must send a telephone warning to Control. Tell them to cease traffic until after our meeting at Middelheim."

With that, Jan made his excuses and went upstairs, wondering how to deal with his problems which threatened to get worse every day.

CHAPTER 7

At The Department of Transport in London

The security conference organised by the Department of Transport in the ugly concrete tower block at No. 2 Marsham Street, London SW1, had been meticulously planned by the Permanent Secretary, after an all too short consultation with the Minister. The P.S. - John Pennywhistle - was thoroughly satisfied with the agenda and the large attendance list. This was always an important test of Ministerial prestige, and had been collated painfully over a period of many weeks after an endless series of slow moving Minutes, telephone calls generating more Minutes, and the usual circulation to all possible addressees of all imaginable discussion points which could, or might conceivably, be considered at such a conference.

Ivor Jones, the Minister, willingly left the organisation and agenda to his P.S. so that he would remain free to consider other more important matters such as the recent suggestion, by one of his local urban constituents, that dog messes on pavements should be cleared away at public expense, but that the offending dog owners should be liable, if found and apprehended, to an on-the-spot fine or sentenced to a spell of public service, clearing up dog messes for example.

So it was that the agenda was built up on a foundation resembling a pile of confetti, rather than expert knowledge or experience of the subject, or adequate consideration of the technical or practical aspects involved.

The meeting started well for the Minister, as he explained

the need for regular consultation on security matters affecting the Channel Tunnel, owing to the recent I.R.A. operation to drive a two ton bomb into the tunnel, a plot foiled when the driver left his deadly vehicle unattended in a lorry park to avoid questioning. He pointed out that with this example of the threat so recently detected, vigilance was essential and security precautions could never be relaxed. He welcomed the participants, and the meeting began with an introduction by the Controller West, George Trent. His tall figure stood out awkwardly over the small lectern.

"Minister, we thank you for arranging this conference here at Marsham Street. We understand your concerns which we share, and we hope to cover considerable ground today. I would also like to thank Monsieur Corbiere, who has come over from Calais especially in order to be here today, for this essentially joint Anglo-French meeting."

The Deputy Controller East, Charles Corbiere, smiled and nodded in his Gallic way. He had been given a pile of briefing notes but found them voluminous without being enlightening - a civil service smokescreen, in his professional opinion, but worth filing in Calais in case the subject matter was aired again.

"My own Deputy, Jack Holmes, could not be here today as he is of course involved in the day-to-day running of the Folkestone Terminal, but he is with us in spirit, I am sure."

The meeting covered ground too familiar to be reported in detail, but the subject was seized upon by ITN news that night. The interview with the Minister was as savage as it was carefully aimed.

"Minister, do you have any faith in the security of the undersea crossing to France, after the recent I.R.A. bomb threat? Is that threat still a factor in your thinking and planning?"

"Certainly, Justin, in fact I was at a security conference this morning at the Department of Transport, where we discussed this very subject in considerable depth. You can rest assured that the security of our fixed link with France is paramount in my mind, and is taken very seriously at my Department."

"But may I remind you, Minister, we have heard that the one thing required to improve security in the Tunnel, code-named Project Brunel, is not being funded by the Government. Are you still able to say that your Department has performed its full part in a matter of such great importance to the security of the nation, and its travelling public?"

"Well, we are constantly reviewing safety measures, I can assure you, and whatever needs to be done will of course be done. I cannot comment on the exact measures, if any, which need our attention, for security reasons."

"Are you saying that the Government will actually be spending money to ensure that Project Brunel will be funded?"

"The answer to your question is highly confidential, and I would prefer to discuss broader issues, but let me remind you that the Channel Tunnel is a joint Anglo-French project, and we are constrained by that. Agreement on the need for funding, and the funds themselves, are a joint matter."

"Can you tell the public when these joint matters will be resolved?"

"I will ensure that the public is informed as soon as negotiations now in progress are completed."

"Thank you Minister. We will hold you to that."

Back in his office next morning, Ivor Jones asked his Deputy Secretary to call his opposite number in Paris and update himself on progress with Project Brunel. This was an ambitious automatic control and rescue system, involving new closed circuit TV connections between Folkestone and Calais, a computer-controlled takeover of all functions between the two terminals in an emergency, and the provision of two special rescue locomotives, one at Folkestone and one at Calais. These had recently been built and tested in the United States, and were designed to run on liquified natural gas stored at a temperature of minus 260 degrees Fahrenheit, so they produced only one tenth of the exhaust emissions created by a typical diesel locomotive. Project Brunel was therefore an expensive, self-contained system, independent of normal tunnel traffic and control measures, to stop and rescue a train either incapacitated in the tunnel, or taken over by terrorists.

The reply that the Minister's Deputy received from Paris was that the French rail working party considered the scheme was still too expensive, and could only be introduced in phases, using the existing back-up diesel locomotives, with their exhaust scrubber wagons, which had only recently been delivered.

Arriving in the House of Commons for Prime Minister's Question Time, the Minister informed the PM of the French update, in case a question was raised - which it duly was.

"Madam Speaker, is the Prime Minister aware of growing disquiet in the country over security arrangements in the Channel Tunnel, and is he taking adequate measures to address this problem, of which his Transport Department is well aware, and has been for some considerable time?"

The Prime Minister handled the question in his usual reassuring manner, interlacing his reply with the stilted Civil Service grammar provided in his written brief on the Despatch Box.

"I can assure the honourable member that we are in close contact with our French opposite numbers over all necessary measures to guarantee adequate security in the Channel Tunnel, and that we are very close to agreement on any and all steps which might be needed to ensure one hundred percent safety for the travelling public."

"Will the Prime Minister now confirm that, although the

Government has never previously contributed to the funding of the Channel Tunnel, this time it will make a proper financial commitment to Project Brunel, the safety measures now urgently required to overcome terrorist attacks on the tunnel and the trains running through it?"

"I am unable as yet to confirm the funding. That will have to await agreement with our French partners as to their financial contribution. At present I have nothing more to say on this matter, which is being kept under constant review by my right honourable friend the Transport Secretary, but the House will be kept fully informed as usual."

When Question Time was over the Minister returned to his office and started to draft a message to his French opposite number, urging him to take a closer interest in Project Brunel, then thought better of it as he remembered his dinner engagement with a certain friend, which took priority over all other, perhaps nobler, thoughts and actions. He telephoned his Permanent Secretary.

"John, could you step along and see me for a moment? Nothing urgent, but I am just leaving."

"Certainly, Minister. Give me a couple of minutes." John Pennywhistle told the Under Secretary he was off to see the Minister, then strode along the passage.

"Ah, good afternoon John. Do please sit down. I apologise for asking you to come at such short notice. It's nothing serious - or rather it is serious but not too serious."

"I understand perfectly, Minister. Were you in the House this afternoon?"

"Exactly, John. That was how the slight problem arose. The PM was asked about the progress of Project Brunel, possibly as a result of my interview on TV last night."

"Yes, I saw that. I don't know why ITN picked it up. Presumably they were prompted by Eurotunnel in the hope of getting public funding - or should I say some public funds - which they haven't been able to get before."

"The rule of no public funding still applies, John. I am sure you realise it cannot be changed at this late stage. Our responsibility must end at the Folkestone transformer station - or rather outside the station - with a commitment to ensure power is provided from the grid. We can't start paying for any equipment - that would need a new Act of Parliament."

"Yes, Minister, but we have urged Eurotunnel on many occasions to improve safety and security. They have had a lot of train stoppages and computer failures, but can't do much more unless you provide funds. Their argument is that it's a matter of national security. Have you anything in mind since your visit to the House?"

"I can only rely on covert funding, through the contingency reserves or the defence budget. But as yet we haven't got agreement from the French side. Can you suggest a way of speeding up their response? Ours may be slow but steady - as we like to portray it - but the PM has asked me to look at Brunel urgently and report in two weeks. Unfortunately I have an important engagement in my constituency this evening, so I will have to leave it with you until tomorrow. The PM thinks we could fund the changes if our French partners will share the cost."

"Minister, I have been thinking." That's a surprise, thought Ivor Jones most uncharitably, because his P.S. could easily out-think the Minister whilst asleep, with his hands tied behind his back.

"My thoughts are these: suppose we got Eurotunnel to stage another stoppage in the tunnel. This time a serious loss of power with lots of passengers stranded. We could call it an exercise. The media would get hold of the story. Public outcry. Another Question in the House. Green light given for funding. Q.E.D."

The Minister appeared perplexed. "*Quod erat demonstrandum*: Quite easily done," explained the P.S. inaccurately.

"The problem is - and thanks for your translation - that the public would have to be compensated for their inconvenience. You know - it's called the Citizen's Charter. If there are leaves on the line the train is late, and the public has to be compensated for travelling by rail - in this country at least."

"Minister, that is not the problem. It need not happen in this country: it can be on our good friends' territory - at the other end of the tunnel. The problem, in my view, is getting the French to pay for Brunel. May I suggest that you have a word with the Controller West, and get him to help to stage manage things on the lines I have indicated?"

The Minister hesitated. "The stoppage might reflect badly on the department, John. Oh, no it wouldn't of course. It would reflect badly on Eurotunnel. Then we could come to the rescue and gain Brownie points for so doing."

"Exactly, Minister."

"Good, so perhaps you would brief my Deputy and work out the details of an approach to the Controller West at Folkestone."

"Certainly, Minister." With that John Pennywhistle departed, wondering whether he had bitten off more than he could chew this time, thereby letting the Minister off yet another barbed hook. In such a way, he reflected, are politics carried on nowadays. The problem would be to convince the French, as the Minister had already discovered. Perhaps an 'exercise' was the only way.

Monsieur Corbiere was not at all convinced when he received the proposition by phone next day.

"As Deputy Controller, I will have to refer to the Controller, who will have to lobby his Minister of Transport, who will have to consult the Prime Minister. We cannot agree to anything in a few weeks, or even months. As for an exercise, as you call it, to stop the trains running, we have already had too many stoppages to even consider arranging another ourselves. Rest assured, that will arrange itself."

The Deputy Secretary could not find any good news for Ivor Jones, the Minister, at the end of the day's wrangling, which had turned into a game of chess with pieces designed for another game altogether, the game of politics rather than railways. But the matter remained urgent, and an answer still had to be found one day. That day was coming soon.

CHAPTER 8

At Middelheim, Near Antwerp

It was a fine morning when three groups of visitors converged on the vast statue collection at Middelheim. Completely lacking an interest in art, they had come furtively, hoping not to be seen. They were all looking for someone else, hence they could hardly avoid being seen by everyone around during their search.

The MI6 Group led by Ken Johnson looked like American gangsters, outfitted in nondescript clothes covered by expensive rainwear with large pockets concealing their extensive equipment. This ranged from a sensitive voice recorder capable of picking up low frequency sound at extreme distances, to a neat machine pistol able to neutralise an unfriendly hominid at thirty paces.

The SVR team, consisting of Victor Krasnov and Galina Svetlov, was drably dressed, as might be expected, and late for the appointment in accordance with an old KGB doctrine for survival.

The Mechelen pair, of Jan Brouwers and Anton Karoly, looked nervously around, and spent some minutes scrutinising every individual arriving at the ticket office. They were watched by Johnson and his group, who had no idea whom to expect, but quite good intuition when it came to shifty underworld characters.

"This looks a likely pair, Octavius," Johnson whispered to the bearer of the voice recorder: "See if you can tune in to them. I will walk away, then you can catch up and see what we have."

Until this moment, no-one had bought a ticket. Like musical chairs when the music stops, somebody had to be the first, then the rush would be on.

Jan and Anton were the first to act. They did so in silence, as pre-arranged. Next were Johnson and his two helpers, equally careful not to give away any hint of their nationality or identity. The two groups stood around awkwardly, waiting for the third, which they were both expecting to arrive. This duly happened at last, and caused adrenalin to flow inside the waiting watchers.

Ken Johnson realised that he had two separate sets of fish to fry as soon as the SVR pair arrived, collected tickets, and wandered off slowly, followed by Jan and Anton.

"A nice day. And the park is not too crowded," said Jan in a clear voice. This was pre-arranged: if it had rained, it was "rather a wet day" and if crowded, the words were to be "the park is quite busy." The prescribed expressions were essential KGB-speak for this operation.

The other pair duly responded: if a nice day the reply was to be "Have you been here before?" or if a wet or cloudy day: "It looks as if it might clear up." So it was that Victor Krasnov responded to signs of fine weather, and the two pairs came together for a brief, apparently casual encounter, before parting. Jan whispered: "See you by the moat in ten minutes," and they moved apart.

Octavius had kept his recorder running, and the gist of the conversation was clearly captured, if not Jan's whispered instructions. But Ken Johnson had sights on his quarry now, and spoke to his second assistant, Aristide Laurent.

"Get a photo of those people without fail, Aristide, even if it takes you away from us. But get on with it. Pretend you are photographing statues or whatever. That's your job now, OK?" Laurent nodded and followed the quartet erratically, pretending to look at works of art on the way.

The SVR quartet re-united at the famous English sculptor Henry Moore's work 'King and Queen', where they conversed with gestures suitable to the occasion, then walked across to the Mechelen sculptor Rik Wouters' statue 'The Mad Maiden', where they agreed to move swiftly on, and meet at the opposite side of the park, by the larger surrealistic works spread out on that side of the road. The red brick structure which Anton had noted before - and described as a house without windows - was decided upon. They arrived half an hour later, by which time both pairs had taken up the appearance of genuine art lovers engrossed in their subject. Ken Johnson decided to follow the Mechelen pair, and was able to shadow them across the road to their intended meeting place.

"I think we are being followed," whispered Jan to Galina. "We had better go back to Number 6."

After a brief consultation with Victor, Galina gave an affirmative sign and the quartet moved off leaving nothing more incriminating than their photographs as evidence - or so they thought.

"Damn!" cursed Ken Johnson, "we've followed them too closely. We'll have to continue the chase. If they go to the car parking area we'll follow them by road." Soon afterwards, they caught sight of Jan getting into a car in the parking area along the roadside, and raced to their own vehicle parked not far behind. With a roar of the engine and a smell of burning tyres, they started to give chase, keeping at a safe distance behind the fast moving getaway car driven by their quarry. After many twists and turns, following the high speed run down the E19 towards Mechelen, they reached the city suburbs, and the quarry turned into the Kazernestraat. By the time Johnson had parked his car by the roadside, the target had disappeared.

"F—k our luck!" cursed Ken again. He tended to be brief, and enjoyed using the four letter vocabulary he preferred to employ when on Her Majesty's service. The other two were amused if not surprised by Ken's grasp of poetry. "I've got an idea," said Laurent. "We know their car number, so we can visit the headquarters of the local Gendarmerie, and trace them that way."

They found out from a passer-by where the HQ of the Gendarmerie was located, then drove there and entered the grey brick building. A fresh-faced young Belgian directed them to the Enquiries desk, behind which a care-worn man suffering from too many hard years of investigative work asked what their business was.

"We are working for the British Intelligence service," said Ken by way of introduction to the man who had ceased to be amazed by anything or anyone. "I can give you proof of that if you wish. We are from London, and we are currently pursuing some people working in this area who may be terrorists. Our information came from a radio message which was picked up in northern Germany and passed on to us. Have you any records of radio broadcasts in this area?"

The Gendarme went away for a few minutes, while the MI6 trio waited and wondered. Then the Gendarme returned.

"Yes, we have some information about radio signals being broadcast from Mechelen, but it is not easy to trace the origin, and we have no idea where they come from. I am sorry, but we cannot help you at the moment."

Johnson leaned over the counter and wrote a car registration number on the message pad in front of him.

"Could you trace a car which we followed here, and which stopped near the Kazernestraat, across the river Dijle?"

"Unfortunately we have no facilities for that. The national register is still being compiled, at the request of Interpol, but it will take another year to complete, when all new licences have been issued. I can put in a request, to see if they have this vehicle on record. Just a minute, please."

The Gendarme obligingly returned a few minutes later,

waving a piece of paper.

"You are in luck. The vehicle was stolen a few days ago in Antwerp. The only problem is, we know the name and address of the owner, but not the thieves of course. I can start a search if you give me proof of your credentials, but our success rate in finding stolen cars does not give us much hope. They usually end up on fire, in a forest, and identification marks are normally removed or destroyed in the fire."

Ken showed the Gendarme his MI6 identity card. "We are in a position to pay for the incidental costs of such a search, but we have to leave for England shortly. Could you send us information to this address?" Johnson wrote down a covert address.

"We will certainly do what we can. I would advise, however, that you might be more fortunate if you make a search locally yourself, and let us know if you are successful. We have discovered that if the scent is allowed to go cold, the bird may have flown - if I may use an English expression." Ken couldn't help smiling at this useful but maladroit combination of two metaphors.

"All right, we will try to locate the vehicle, and keep you informed, but if you do find out anything, please let us know at the address I gave you. I expect that we may meet again before long."

Ken was starting to enjoy the mission after all. If not exactly a knighthood, at least something might come out of it. He hustled his charges into the car, then drove off across the Dijle to where he thought the other car had disappeared. It was nowhere to be seen, and Ken once again cursed his luck in the usual four-letter vocabulary, regretting the short burst of enthusiasm at MI6 headquarters which had led to his presence at this fiasco. Or was it a fiasco? He realised they had photographs of the quarry, but the Gendarmes might not be able to trace them from photographs - but could they?

Perhaps they would make an effort, and check half the driving licences in Belgium against the photographs inside. Maybe some of the terrorists were local. Ken decided to press on. They drove around the area, looking in side streets, until finally they realised that the car could now be inside a garage somewhere, or anywhere for that matter. It was time to be more scientific.

There was just time to drive down to Calais, catch the last shuttle train to Folkestone, and reach London that evening. It was dark and raining, and Ken did not expect a friendly response from Allan Gunn on their return to MI6. They drove in silence to the Calais terminal, and past the brightly lit signs, so clinical and solid, unlike the messy operation he was engaged in. At the British Customs, a wave of Ken's official pass saw them on their way towards the loading area, beyond the overbridges.

"Which is our loading bridge?" asked Ken. "Number 2 loads the front of the shuttle, it's signed over there," said Aristide. So they drove down to the platform, and were waved into the shiny aluminium shuttle wagon.

"Aristide, do you think you have some decent photos of those four? Can we see your pictures in the morning, then we can send them to Interpol? They just might have a line on one or other of those jokers."

"Of course, Ken. I expect to have all four on film. My Olympus is fool-proof. You just point and shoot. A perfect result every time, as the advertisements say. The focus and shutter are automatic."

"OK, then I'll drop you off at the photo labs when we get to London, and we'll have a quick look. Octavius, your voice recordings may not be conclusive now, but putting the two together we might get Interpol to make a proper search."

Octavius nodded. "Yes, I haven't played them back yet, but we can listen to the tapes when you are ready."

They had reached the huge Calais terminal just in time for

a practice alert, and spent the next half hour in the stationary train, waiting for any news. "You know," Johnson exclaimed, "the security here is amazing. The place is full of officials in and out of uniform, some of them armed, others with radio sets. The place is like a concentration camp." Then he stiffened. "Look, we may be onto something here. The radio intercepts which sent us off on this wild goose chase spoke of a high state of security. Where else could that be, except here at this terminal?"

"You could be right" said Octavius, the serious thinker of the pair, and a fluent Flemish speaker. "Let us listen to these recordings first, but I agree that you will never find a higher state of security than this, except at Fort Knox."

At last the shuttle train glided silently into the tunnel, with profuse apologies for the delay from the control staff, speaking over the public announcement system. Then the only view from the windows was of an interminable cooling pipe on the tunnel wall, lit up by lights every few seconds, otherwise there was no sensation of movement. The train quietly gathered speed in the darkness.

"Right, Octavius, can we hear your recordings?"

"Just a minute, I will turn up the volume." The recorder whirred...

"—Come over this way, Victor, and I will give you some directions. We will have to move over to the statues by the old house if we want to be alone.... OK we are in your hands...let us go over to this one, the King and Queen, by the moat... I think we are being followed. Let us move to the next statue and see...Yes we are being followed...Can we meet over the road?... there is this large abstract brick building... OK we will follow... I think we had better move again... Galina, I think we should go to Mechelen, then we can discuss matters more privately—"

The recordings tailed off into mush and then silence.

Ken spoke. "I think that was mainly our Belgian, judging

from the accent, and they are based in Mechelen. He must have been in charge. Someone replied twice, with a distinctly Russian accent. No-one else spoke, you notice. So we managed to get two of them, a Belgian and a Russian. Well done, Octavius. And the photos will be very useful. If we ever come back here, or the French DST security people can put them together, that will get us all firmly on the trail."

"Those voice characteristics are unique, you know," said Octavius. "It is impossible to alter or conceal them effectively. A court of law could be shown the printout of those voices, and convict on the evidence we have collected."

"Anyway, we came but did not conquer - as yet," said Ken, more cheerfully now. "We had better work out the next step before we reach London. If the Gendarmes could see the photographs - particularly of the Belgian - and hear the voices, they might be able to find them. They seemed to know about the radio transmissions, but couldn't pinpoint anyone in particular. With our evidence, they might have a better chance."

Suddenly the train stopped abruptly. The public address system began to speak:

"Passengers are asked to bear with us for a few moments. There has been a fire alarm, and we will keep you informed. The train stops automatically in such cases, but there is nothing to worry about."

A few minutes later the train continued on to Folkestone without incident. Ken Johnson was relieved to be back, until he realised how much work had to be done before he could close the case.

CHAPTER 9

In Brussels and Mechelen

Major Victor Krasnov of the SVR arrived at Mechelen in a mood of ill humour verging on paranoia. A simple mission to make contact with his agents had turned into a farcical and ignominious car chase.

A mousy, furtive, even shifty relic of the old apparatchik system, with busy hands and mobile eyes, Krasnov was obviously nervous. He had seen better days, and his promotion in the past had relied heavily on his habit of spying on friends and colleagues, then using them as an excuse for his failures. He liked the good life his job provided, but secretly, when he could get away from head office. His victim this time was Jan Brouwers, the senior SVR agent at Mechelen.

"I had intended to discuss our plans here," he announced weightily on arrival at Number 6, Donkerlei, "and they are of great importance, but security seems totally out of control here. So I will have a few words now with Anton and Igor before I leave for Brussels. I want you to stay here, Brouwers, in case there are any more problems, and I will take Anton and Igor with me, also Galina. They can come back here tonight. If anyone questions Galina's presence here in Mechelen, you are to say that she is Anton's girl-friend on a visit from Poland - nobody can tell the difference between Russian and Polish in Belgium. Also, Galina speaks Polish, but not German."

So it was that Victor discussed the state of security with

Anton, the coach driver, not the leader of the section, Jan. Then he pressed Igor to explain why he could not guarantee transmissions from Donkerlei. "Do you think you will have to move?" he asked.

"No. That would be very difficult, and attract suspicion, particularly with Jan's friend, the landlord. His name is Johan Diedericks, and he does not realise that Igor is staying here, only myself as driver of the Pegasus coach. It would be fatal to attract his attention at this time. Besides, a move would break up the team."

"In that case, make sure the landlord doesn't find out anything," commanded Victor tersely. He had already wondered if the team's days ought to be limited after today's experiences. "Now we will go off to have dinner at the Grand Place in Brussels, then you can bring Galina back here. I would like her to continue the discussions until I return tomorrow morning. You can collect me just before nine from the Novotel Brussels near the Grand Place, at 120 Rue du Marché aux Herbes. After our meeting here in Mechelen you can take me to the station, and then get rid of the car."

The four duly drove off, leaving Jan to savour his sudden fall from grace. The strain was becoming intense, because he had not seen Johan Diedericks for several weeks, and the fact that Johan did not realise that Number 6 housed an extra lodger was beginning to seem a problem without an obvious solution. They might soon be discovered, with incalculable consequences for all three of them.

On arrival in Brusssels, Anton parked the car along the side of a suburban road near the Independence Monument at the Place des Martyrs, and the quartet set out for the Grand Place, eagerly in the case of the two Russians, who had never seen its splendour and charms before.

Victor was in a slightly better frame of mind. The good life beckoned, and he spoke cheerfully for the first time since he had arrived in Belgium.

"Galina, I am sure you will enjoy the sights here tonight, and also the cuisine. Belgium is famous for its food, you know. There are some good little restaurants near the Grand Place, apparently, and I have been recommended one in Pepper Street - the Champignon. So we can book a table there, and have a look at the illuminations, before going back for a well deserved meal."

"That would be wonderful, Victor," enthused Galina, "we could also talk freely there."

"Exactly, Galya, although we will have to be careful with the others present."

Galina was a stylishly beautiful lady of middle age, rather buxom as befitted years of satisfactory employment with the old KGB, and positive in manner, but charming at the same time. Born in the Ukraine, a fiercely independent country, she came from a good family. Efficient and charismatic, always well dressed, she was a role model for the new Russian woman - the sophisticated lady who had replaced the old labouring stereotype.

The vista of the Grand Place as they approached along the west side was alive with sights and sounds. The jugglers, beggars, magicians and musicians were all cheerfully entertaining the foreign visitors. Above and beyond the human fringes of the square rose the floodlit town offices and rich burghers houses belonging to the old families of Brussels, when past times were the present. Galina, who had only left Moscow once before, for a quick visit to Mechelen, was amazed to see the display of wealth and culture before them.

"Victor, this is beautiful, is it not? Saint Petersburg must have looked like this before" - she caught her breath but could not stop the thoughts from turning into words - "the Bolshevik Revolution. Of course, it is all show and no substance, as we can see. Obviously nobody lives here. It is all a display to catch the tourists." Secretly, she was lost for words now, having never seen the glories of European architecture before - that was denied to all ordinary Russians who were not members of the upper layer of the Nomenklatura - the new class created by the Communists establishment, which still persisted stubbornly in the new Russia. Moscow was drab and ugly by comparison.

At the Restaurant des Champignons the quartet was ushered to a table set with flowers and surrounded with an aroma of good food - not the sort which Anton and Igor were used to at all - nor Victor and Galina except at special KGB functions in days gone by. Galina was again in full flow. "This is really nice, don't you think?" she asked of the other three. Even Victor had to admit that he was impressed, but he quickly turned to the business in hand, which had been postponed so long.

"Galina, what did you think of our reception today? I thought we were being followed, but I can't be sure. I wonder whether it was stage managed correctly. We could have walked into a trap at Middelheim. Do you think that our visit was anticipated? If so, how could anyone have known? Perhaps I have imagined the whole thing."

"I don't know, Victor. Perhaps we can sleep on that, and discuss it again tomorrow, after we have spoken to Jan again. He, after all, was responsible for all the arrangements. You might ask him some questions in the morning, before you go."

"Do you think," Victor whispered to Galina, "that Jan is totally reliable?"

"Of course," she whispered. "But" - and she gave him a kick under the table - "we can't discuss that here and now. Be careful." Luckily Anton and Igor were not listening, as they were busy dissecting the day's events - the trip to Middelheim and back, the unsatisfactory meeting in the park, and their high speed return to Mechelen, shaking off their imagined pursuers. They had no doubts about their employers in the

SVR who had come to see them. Many former KGB agents had suffered from delusions of security: it only took one failure - unless you were a trustworthy KGB agent with a solid history of active and successful duty - and you were in line for a visit to the interrogation rooms at the Lubyanka. It was not an experience many would like to contemplate, unless solid evidence in their defence was at hand, and quickly.

"Anton, you are in good spirits tonight. Tell me what you think of this project, as far as it has gone." Victor was probing again.

"The project has not really begun, Victor, and I think we have not yet found out what we are up against. I went to Calais a few days ago, and had great difficulty getting into the rail terminal without a ticket. Security is very tight. We will have to go again, of course, but decided to wait for your visit first. If we go more than once there is a chance that we may be compromised." Victor nodded.

"Anton, excuse me for asking, but did your family not leave Warsaw during the Patriotic War as prisoners of the German SS?"

Anton swallowed, then steadied himself. "Yes, they did. I imagine the suffering was no different from the fate of so many others," he replied distantly. "Were you involved in that hell on earth?"

"No, it happened before my time," replied Victor. "But I can imagine how it felt to a young boy. I suppose it robbed him of his childhood, and his future. At least under the Bolsheviks that was spared, unless you backed the wrong side." Victor smiled weakly. "It is true that the drastic purges and the Great Patriotic War which followed dispossessed and destroyed millions of people. We have had to make many compromises on the way to our salvation, and they were all painful but useful, and ultimately successful - don't you agree? I hope you can understand that Russian view of history, bearing in mind our earlier experiences under the Czar's despotic regime."

"I think so," replied Anton, but in reality he was thinking of the future now, not the past. "Victor, I believe we will need more guidance to complete this mission. It is not easy, and I hope that someone is in charge of the planning. We will need some instructions, you know."

"The Spetznatz forces will take care of that," said Victor, "as soon as you are ready to hand over to them. That means that you will have finished your job, and they can start theirs." Anton's reaction to this news was interrupted by Igor, who was listening.

"Will we be finished then, Victor?"

"I cannot tell. Obviously we have to operate on several fronts at the same time. Eventually you will hand over and" - Victor paused, trying to find suitable words to break the news - "and others will take up the torch for Mother Russia, so to speak." For all his bourgeous background, Victor possessed an earthy intellect that few could criticise.

Anton himself was a veteran of many KGB plots, counterplots, successes and failures, and he had a good inkling of what it meant to relinquish the torch at too early a stage in a delicate operation of this size. Silence was more important than actions if you were a member of the supporting cast in a KGB enterprise.

"I think I see what you mean," he said without any feelings at all. The room had suddenly become cold, in spite of the flickering candles and warmth from the kitchen.

"What Victor is trying to say," Galina added as helpfully as she could, "is that we are all servants of the SVR, and should not expect any special favours." Victor nodded, but he was actually thinking of various favours which Galina had granted him in the past - he was her boss, after all.

"You are quite right, Galya" - he used the shortened version of her name, a term of endearment in Russia and

79

elsewhere, by mistake - "we cannot expect to earn our bread without blood. I trust that does not seem too unreasonable. But to sum it up, we may have to proceed on two or even more fronts with this operation. I cannot be more specific at this moment." At this stage he truly had no more idea than they of what the future held in store for the enterprise.

After paying the exhorbitant bill, the quartet moved off up the narrow, thronged street and headed north towards the suburban road where the car had been left. In the dark it was hard to find, and they searched for at least ten minutes before the truth finally dawned: the car had gone. "A thousand curses!" mouthed Victor to anyone listening. "I have left my overnight case in that damn car. Keep on walking, in case they are waiting for us to return. We will have to watch from a distance, and then leave if nothing happens. On second thoughts, we should go now, and hope they have taken the car far away to search it. It is too dark to see here."

"What did you leave in the bag? Anything that would lead them back to us?" Anton was alarmed now.

"No. Only a label might be found, from a Moscow clothing store. That would be bad enough, but there is no sign of identification, of course. We must keep away from the area. Galina, you take Anton and Igor back to Mechelen by taxi, and I will make my own arrangements to get there tomorrow morning. Now, I will walk to my hotel alone. I will say goodnight, and remember - you know nothing about the stolen car."

Victor strode off into the night without another word. After all, Galina was an old paramour. One must not waste time when in Brussels with no pyjamas. The other three eventually found a taxi to take them back to Mechelen. Arriving late, they asked to be dropped at the Horseshoe, and walked down to Number 6, Donkerlei. Jan came to answer the chimes.

"You have been later than I expected. Is all well?"

Anton replied quietly. "We have lost the car, Jan. It was stolen from the street while we were at the restaurant."

"That will save us some trouble - but can it be traced back here? Did you leave anything inside?"

"Yes. Victor's overnight bag. He swears there is nothing incriminating in it, but who knows? Perhaps the car will be returned to its owner in Antwerp - there is nothing to connect it with us here in Mechelen. So the police will have to contact Interpol about Victor's bag - if they find anything they can use."

"Unfortunately" - Igor's voice chipped in severely - "Victor says he left a shirt with the label of a well known Moscow store used by the *nomenklatura*. That could be a problem."

Galina spoke drowsily. "I suggest we all go to bed - it is late. How many bedrooms do you have here?"

"Three, but you are welcome to share," said Anton and Igor simultaneously. Galina decided that Jan would be a better proposition. He was more her type, and besides she needed to pry more deeply into his motives. She accepted Jan's offer, and went upstairs with him.

"Please, Galina, have the bed. I will sleep on the floor. It won't be the first time."

"Certainly not, Jan, I will sleep on the floor, with a blanket," replied Galina stoutly. "I too have past experiences, and find my brain works better when it is deprived of comfort."

They slept for a few hours, until Jan started to have a nightmare.

"Are you alright?" called Galina.

"I'm sorry, it was just a bad dream."

"About your past life during the war?"

"Yes. My aunt's house was bombed after the allies had landed - it was destroyed by the allies. Isn't that crazy? I was homeless again."

Galina stirred uneasily. "This floor is rather hard, Jan. Do you mind if I share the mattress with you? I will try to be quiet, but it is a bit cold down here."

"You are most welcome," said Jan, waking up to the idea of sharing his bed with a member of the old KGB. It was all above board - no problem, he was nearly sure. Or was it a possible trap? Galina climbed into the bed, and Jan felt her cool body close to his. He pulled her a little closer. "I hope you will be alright now, Galina," thinking of Mother Russia and her endlessly splendid examples.

"Don't worry about me, Jan. I am more worried about you," she whispered. "Victor is inclined to think that you are not reliable." She leaned over him. "Are you?"

"My dear Galya - may I call you that? - of course you can rely on me to serve the cause until they decide my work is no longer needed. Perhaps we could talk about that tomorrow?"

Galya's hand strayed slightly. "I am sure you are loyal, Jan. The other two are very fond of you, and grateful for your help."

"Galya, I sometimes feel we have the world in our hands at times like this. Do you not feel that, in many ways?" Scenes from the battle of Waterloo lingered in his mind.

"I think I know what it feels like, and just now especially." Galina gave him a squeeze between the legs and rolled over towards him. He gave her a gentle hug in return, and they moved together in the middle of the bed. Still half asleep but acting decisively, Galina began to exercise the prerogative of KGB officials abroad, with more junior agents of the opposite sex. They were assumed to be available and no questions were permitted before, during or afterwards. Jan felt himself sinking into a dangerous but exhilarating trance with his beautiful conqueror, who was so calm but masterful. He did not - indeed could not - object to an ardent lesson in Russian love-making. As a bachelor, he had no objections at all, and entered eagerly into the moments of abandonment which awaited them both.

"You are really just a beautiful boy who lost his mother," crooned Galina softly.

"Perhaps, but I am so glad I have found another, like you," breathed Jan into the inviting gap between her soft, yielding breasts, which surrounded his face, and his whole psyche, like angels wings. She took up a dominant position over him, they coupled, and his passion welled up. The spasms of two overpowering orgasms sent them both into a tired but dreamless sleep without nightmares, in their new happiness at the unlikely love-nest of Number 6, Donkerlei.

In the morning the discussion resumed on a serious note. Galina had reverted to her businesslike other self as she set about probing the recent activities of the three residents of Number 6, Donkerlei. It soon became evident that time had been wasted.

"Anton, you say that you drive the Pegasus coach, but how often is that, and where do you go?"

"I am employed part time, and there is usually little warning of where we are going. The business is a small one, owned by Johan Diedericks, our landlord, and he specialises in mystery tours - that is, the tours are usually a mystery even to the driver until the day they take place. But they are very popular. The coach stops to take on passengers in the Grote Markt near St Rombout's tower every day, with a different itinerary. There are two drivers, and we take turns, but we don't always know where we are going until the evening before, or who is going to drive."

"That sounds interesting," Galina noted. "But can you make suggestions about where to go? For instance, could you drive to Calais and through the tunnel to southeast England. I hear that Kent is a favourite destination for French tourists, and they like to visit the cathedral at Canterbury."

"I think we can always make suggestions, as I have told

83

Jan. He is our official contact with Diedericks, and he gave me this job," replied Anton. "Before I forget, today is Monday, and it is possible that Diedericks will come here to see if all is well for our next trip tomorrow, to Bruges and Antwerp."

Galina was startled. "He can't come here and find four people in the house - that is quite impossible! It is nearly 9.30 now, and Victor might arrive at any minute. If your friend arrives, you had better think of a good way of keeping him out. Or, perhaps we should go to your Horseshoe café now, rather than risk it. You can stay here Anton, and send Victor on to the café without attracting attention."

Jan, Galina and Igor walked to the Horseshoe just in time, as Diedericks drove up to the house a few minutes later. Anton was there to meet him. Victor had not yet arrived from Brussels.

"Good morning, Anton," said Diedericks. "I have come to tell you that we need you tomorrow, for the trip to Bruges and Antwerp. Is Jan here?"

"Good morning, Johan. How nice to see you. I'm afraid that Jan has gone out for a short time, to get a paper or something. Shall I come to the office later?"

"Yes, that would be best. The secretary is there, and she will give you details of the trip. The usual start time of ten in the morning, I believe. How was your trip to Waterloo?"

Anton was by now getting worried about Victor's imminent arrival, but said nothing. The arrangement was that if the red light over the door was switched on, it was not safe to enter until the light was extinguished.

"We had an interesting time as usual, Johan. I was struck this time by the narrowness of the victory over the French, and how the antagonists have kept on changing over the centuries."

"You are so right, Anton. And did the guide mention that Marshal Blucher nearly lost his way to the battlefield? It was a miracle that he arrived at all. But in these modern times I think the world is beginning to change again. Deep forces are at work, in my opinion, bringing France, Belgium and Britain closer together. You see, France is again overshadowed by Germany, and faces the dilemma of its declining power once more, like Britain. It is absolutely necessary that France and Britain remain united in future, politically and geographically. The same applies to Belgium of course. But we now have the Channel tunnel to provide a timely solution to the problem. Perhaps we should consider picking up French tourists and taking them through the tunnel to Kent and beyond. We could get another coach if that is a success, and then you could work full time."

"That sounds a fine idea, Johan. It would suit me well." Anton was absolutely delighted with the prospect of working full time for Pegasus Travel. "I have heard that the French like to visit Dover and Canterbury, and Kent is of course known as the garden of England. In fact London is only an hour up the autoroute from Folkestone, apparently."

"If you can find out about travelling through the tunnel, we could try a pilot trip to Dover, Anton. I suggest you talk to the booking office and visit the terminal at Calais some time."

"Certainly. I am ready at any time that suits you."

Just then, Victor Krasnov arrived at the front door, and the carillon chime rang out a message of danger.

"Excuse me for a moment, please." Anton went to the door and switched on the red light. Victor hesitated for a short time, and then walked up to the Horseshoe café, where he duly found the other three waiting for him. A few minutes later Anton arrived at the café with profuse apologies.

Victor Krasnov seemed tired, as well he might be, and was only interested now in finding a safe area to debrief the SVR trio.

"Where can we go now, Jan? I only have an hour to get to

the train station. What is your opinion about the project now?"

Anton interjected before Jan could reply. "Victor, Johan Diedericks, the owner of Pegasus Travel, has just asked me to visit the Calais terminal and find out all about it, so that he can send his coaches on trips through the tunnel to England. I am afraid that kept me at the house longer than I intended."

Jan was delighted at the news. He turned to Victor and offered to go with Anton, and bring back full details of the terminal.

"Yes but how do we manage to communicate, with all this trouble over radio signals?" - Victor was indicating again that he had nearly finished with the services of the three Mechelen agents.

Jan looked at Galina. "May I suggest that you send Galina here again to collect a final report in writing, with our recommendations. I could contact her by letter, or better still by phone." Jan used his most insistent tone of voice, and Galina readily agreed. "Yes, I think we had better forget the radio and try more personal contact, such as Jan has proposed." Jan nodded rather too enthusiastically for his own good.

"OK. Expect a visit within seven to ten days. Use this telephone number and address to contact Galina." He scribbled on a piece of paper. "But let us be quite clear about one thing. The KGB is riding on this plan, and expects some definite results very soon. Then they will send a Spetznatz team to complete their own survey and make the final plan. All this must be completed within three weeks at most. Now, we must go back. Come along, Galina, will you get your things together?"

Galina and Jan went back together to Donkerlei, and climbed upstairs to collect Galina's sparse belongings. "Well done, Jan. Things are looking better now. I will come and see you as soon as you are ready with your report."

"That will be very soon, Galya, be sure. We cannot keep the KGB - or anyone else - waiting, can we?" He gave her a long kiss and a hug, and she was gone, to Russia with Victor, her old love.

CHAPTER 10

In Mechelen and The Tunnel

Johan Diedericks felt uncomfortable after his visit to Donkerlei. He left with the impression that Anton had been evasive, and there was an atmosphere he could not put his finger on. He had noticed a smell of perfume in the house, which at that time of day seemed strange. He himself was unmarried, and preferred solitude to female company. When his mother died she had left him the business, which he eventually sold. He had numerous friends in Mechelen, and one of his new interests was in membership of the local Special Action Committee - an undercover constabulary which watched out for subversion, and was only responsible to the Directorate Chief at Mechelen. As yet his suspicions had not been fully aroused, and he did not know about the visit of the Gendarmes to Number 6, Donkerlei. Jan had not given his name to the police as their landlord, because he was the legal tenant. This was unfortunate, because the Gendarmes wrote to Diedericks at his office, and he had never before heard of the matter which concerned them:

To the Owner at: Number 6, Donkerlei
We are conducting a search for illegal radio transmissions
in your area, and in case you can help we would be grateful
if you could come to this office within ten days to discuss the
matter. If you have already received this letter, please ignore
it.
(signed)   *Superintendent*
Gendarmerie van Busleydenstraat

Johan was not unduly concerned. The notice arrived at a busy time, and was obviously widely distributed, as the photo-copy was fuzzy. He decided to ask Jan about it next time they met, but time had passed and he had not done so.

Meanwhile the wheels of chance were turning and bets could be placed. By now, Allan Gunn of MI6 had contacted his opposite number in the French DST, and given him sufficient information to activate a special project. Although the research team had plenty of other work to do, the task assigned was important enough to keep computers constantly on line, recording and comparing information received in London and Paris. It was not long before the link-up with London produced a set of photographs and voice prints, both unknown to the DST, and therefore interesting. Nevertheless the paperchase at the DST office in Paris, which was cranked up to a high level of activity, and potentially boded ill for Jan, Anton and Igor, would not automatically succeed in its aim - it would always be clogged with some form of paper paralysis, probably at a critical time.

In Moscow, a special meeting of the Defence Council heard from the retiring Deputy Prime Minister, Yevgeny Gorshkov, who had been instrumental in creating oil and gas fields in Siberia during the past 25 years and was now an important figurehead and capitalist thinker, that he did not support any further moves in the KGB's plan to destroy the tunnel. He opposed Operation Kingdom, as it was now known, because he wanted to complete further trade links with Britain, and had no faith in the old-fashioned ideas at the heart of the hidebound Soviet military regime. He had been born in the early 20's in the Donetsk Province of the Ukraine, and had trained as a railway engineer in Kiev, which was overrun by the Nazis in 1942. Before that he had been a member of the Youth Section of the Komsomol in Moscow, and later became the Minister for Oil and Gas Enterprises. Eventually he supervised construction of the highly profitable pipelines to the West. Such a prominent ex-Minister could not possibly be disregarded, particularly by the newly re-elected President, so the word went out, officially at least, that detente with the West must be maintained intact for reasons of trade and investment.

The KGB, unfortunately, was not listening to the short term aims of politicians: it seldom did. Its aims were always long term. Plans had to be made irrespective of the type of government in power, and they had to be kept ready for implementation.

The Spetznatz team was now ready to move to Mechelen for a briefing, and to take up further exploratory work, as soon as the word was given. They had already studied details of the Channel tunnel, and two men had visited it, disguised as lorry drivers, during the past two months. This was the normal method of reconnaissance practised by the Soviet Army, and had yielded rich results during the cold war attacks on the Nato countries. By now, an extremely good knowledge of the tunnel's weaknesses had been gained, partly with the help of a mole in Transmanche-Link - the tunnel's builders. The Mechelen SVR team had recently arranged a date for a pilot trip through the tunnel, and so the grey cells at KGB headquarters decided to send the Spetznatz group to Mechelen disguised as tourists, in order to make a clandestine trip through the tunnel with Pegasus Travel. Galina Svetlov was detailed to accompany the group, and now she was eager to see what would happen. The thought that the world might be in her and Jan's hands was beginning to occupy her mind again.

In London, the MI6 team headed by Ken Johnson had decided to visit Mechelen once more, to see if any progress had been made by the Gendarmerie in tracing the stolen car. They duly arrived on a day visit, and were told that progress had been made, as one of the car thieves was known to be Russian, and his fingerprints had been photographed, with three other sets. They had continued their search for a clandestine radio broadcaster, and if any further transmissions took place they could probably pinpoint the origin and institute a more thorough search. The scene appeared set for further progress in tracking down the Mechelen plotters, with the aid of Ken's voice-prints which they had just received. So the search had been taken up by Interpol and the French DST, whose solid bureaucratic tendency meant that from now on information had to flow around the triangle in both directions, creating more and more paperwork.

As always, the DST was a principal power in the land, to whom Presidents came for help, and they were not about to surrender their influence to others. The Controller East at Calais, Jean Moris, was informed that extra vigilance had been demanded in northern France, after the discovery of a group of minor terrorists who might be plotting a bank robbery or similar crime in Belgium, and these miscreants seemed to have Russian connections. The advice to Moris was intended to help him to detain the robbers if they should travel through the tunnel to the safety of England or Ireland - the latter was known to be a common destination for proceeds from bank robberies in Europe. In addition a key member of the DST was despatched to the Calais terminal to assist the Controller with any further security measures which might be needed. He was a young and active careerist named Phillipe Villeneuve, who was descended from an illustrious former head of the DST. His appointment to the Calais terminal proved important and timely, although it could never be said that any one security measure would distract the operators of the tunnel from their primary task. This had always been simply and urgently defined - to get European bottoms onto Eurotunnel seats. Any distinctions between friendly and unfriendly customers had largely disappeared after the rival ferry operators declared war on the tunnel, and sent their largest and latest cruise ships into the narrow waterway, promising 'an experience, a cruise, a holiday before the holiday'. The channel tunnel balance sheet was so shaky that nothing else mattered.

Villeneuve's job was to keep in touch with the Deputy Controller East, and gradually create a tougher regime for possible subversives. It had always been recognised that there was a long term threat to the tunnel, but nothing positive had been done until the mysterious radio messages had been noticed, followed by the MI6 expedition and the finding of the stolen car in Brussels. Now the hunt for terrorists took on a new urgency, even if the French hierarchy at Calais found the whole idea contrary to their business sense of the trading bottom line. A golden year beckoned in cross-channel travel, with the advent of the weather-proof tunnel system, so sleek, modern and rapid, so integrated into the transport system for the Europe of the future, which was now a reality. An endless stream of revenue could be expected, particularly after the tragic ferry disaster in the Baltic, when over 900 lives had been lost, and the unique efficiency of travel under the channel would be apparent at any moment - assuming there was no threat to the tunnel itself. That threat, although treated seriously, could never be contained, so it had to be endured ... as the current thinking went.

Hence it was that the typical - and not undeserved - French belief in their superiority over matters technical clashed with the typically English view of their own solid practicality, leaving the field open to an attack from the French side of the tunnel this time.

The Spetznatz team duly arrived at Mechelen, with Galina Svetlov acting as supervisor and guide. They were all housed in the Hotel Aurora, chosen by Victor Krasnov because he thought that their combined efforts might herald a new dawn for the old Soviet Union - an idea shared by many others in the new Russia who were of an optimistic disposition.

Galina phoned No 6 Donkerlei as soon as they arrived, and requested that Jan should come over to the hotel to meet the visitors. He took a taxi and arrived with a certain amount of foreboding. The plan seemed to be moving forward too quickly now, but he could do nothing to stop it.

"Good morning, Galina, how are you?" said Jan at the sight of his new friend in the bright foyer of the hotel.

"Very well, Jan, but please remember we are working members of a team with business to do, and must not appear too friendly. The meeting will be upstairs in room 262. Come with me." She took him to the elevator, and up to the room where three men were seated and waiting. Galina introduced them briefly.

"This is Jan Brouwers comrades, our SVR chief in Mechelen. Jan, may I introduce our three friends from the Spetznatz, whose real names you do not need to know. They are willing to be known as" - she waved her arm from left to right - "Alain, Bernard and Charles: A, B and C. In fact those will be their names from now on, as far as you are concerned. Alain is in charge of the team."

The three men nodded. They seldom spoke, but their evident physical fitness made it clear that they were from a special force, not ordinary mortals. The leader was a thick-set, blue eyed man who exhuded strength and determination. He came from a poor farming background in the Ukraine, but had made up for it in his army career. A bachelor because the army became his life and wife, he had excelled at physical sports and was attached to the old Communist regime which had given him everything he needed.

"Let us get down to business," said Galina briskly to her four charges. "The trip to Folkestone will be tomorrow, is that not right? And at what time will it start? And what more can you tell us about the trip, Jan?"

"We are going to take a party of tourists from the Grote Markt here in Mechelen to Dover via the tunnel, leaving at ten in the morning as usual. I will accompany you and explain what is happening. We will sit in the back of the coach, so that we can talk, and our usual guide will speak to the tourists over the loudspeaker system. When we get to Calais we will board the shuttle train, and go through the tunnel to the Folkestone terminal. Then we will drive to Dover, which is only a few kilometres away, and visit the town and the Castle. This is a trial run for Pegasus Travel. Then we will have lunch at a restaurant at the Folkestone terminal, so that you can see it better. The two terminals have exactly the same design, so you will have three chances to see the layout before we return to Calais and Mechelen."

"That sounds excellent, Jan," said Galina. "Is there anything else to be said now?"

"Only that our friends A, B and C should be dressed as tourists and appear to be relaxed and on holiday. Photographs will be in order, but perhaps not too obviously. There may be a need for identification of the passengers, but that is very lax, and Pegasus will take care of it.

Then we will have a debriefing here at Mechelen afterwards, and the rest is up to the special forces," said Galina with obvious satisfaction. "They will prepare their own report, of course."

"Good," said Jan finally, "so I will see you four at the Grote Markt tomorrow at ten in the morning. But please do not be late - that would draw attention to your group, and might cause a problem."

"Don't worry," said Galina, "I will make sure these three

fine specimens of manhood are on time." She indicated that the meeting was over for Jan. He seemed less than pleased that Galina was being left with three fine examples of male humanity until the morning.

"Now, I will come back with you to Donkerlei, Jan, to see what new information your friends have obtained," she announced.

"Certainly, Galina - I will go and get a taxi." Jan was more than relieved, and the two of them arrived by taxi at the dark lane in the late morning. Jan's advances in the taxi were not welcome, and Galina hissed in his ear: "Jan, another time and place, and certainly not in public if you please. Thank you." She was being dominant again, as was her right.

They found Anton already briefed about the Pegasus coach trip for the following day, and Igor was to be left behind as usual. He was not pleased by the news which Galina brought him.

"Igor, as we cannot continue to communicate by radio, I have been asked to say that you will have to return to Moscow when we have completed our visit to the tunnel, and said goodbye to our three Spetznatz friends. In fact they may escort you back, as they have an extra ticket."

Igor's face turned pale. Anyone summoned back to Moscow these days could not be certain of his future at all: it might be at the whim of a senior KGB officer who felt that the agent was no longer needed. Budgets were very tight now. But Igor had already decided not to go back to Moscow.

"I would like a little more time to prepare for the trip back, Galina. Can you try to arrange an extension?"

"I will ask our friends if they can fix that, but I cannot promise it, Igor."

Next morning the five plotters met up with Anton at the departure point for the coach trip, at the Grote Markt. About twenty more genuine tourists were waiting. Anton ushered them on board, and introduced their guide. The Spetnatz men maintained a discreet silence while the guide spoke over the intercom, then the coach drew away towards the E19 autoroute to Brussels, Gent and Calais. In the rear of the coach, the five subversive passengers enjoyed their drive along the smooth highway, and within three hours the coach drew in to the imposing Coquelles terminal..

The atmosphere was electric as they craned forward and sideways to look at every detail of the enormous facility. The atmosphere of welcome to the tourist created initially by the large notice boards soon gave way to bustle and clinical efficiency, as huge numbers of vehicles arriving at the terminal were split up and marshalled into the different routes to the tunnel for cars, coaches, caravans and heavy trucks. The coach was soon on its way to the ticket control, where Anton had the booking details ready, and then to the security check, where all passengers had to disembark for the luggage to be looked at briefly. Then the passengers were motioned to board their vehicle, and were on their way past wire fences, security guards and their dogs, and more guides, to the loading bridge. The coach was halted for a short while, its way blocked by a queue of traffic waiting to board the gleaming aluminium shuttle train stretched out below them.

"This is your best view, Galina," said Jan, putting a hand excitedly on her knee." You can see the whole boarding area from here. In a few minutes we will go down the ramp and drive into the shuttle wagon. Then you will see nothing until we come out into the light at Folkestone. But remind our three alphabet friends that they have to be prepared for spot checks of their passports and nationality during the journey. They must produce their passports and say they will be returning the same day. Otherwise there may be a problem." Galina nodded. "And can any of them speak the local languages? I mean, French or Flemish?" Galina shook her head, the fair hair swishing into Jan's face, the perfume alluring. "No, but you can handle that Jan, I am sure. We are all going to rely on you when we need you."

Back at Donkerlei, Igor was alone with his thoughts of a journey to Moscow and its endless bad weather and social problems when the door chime was activated. Johan had come to call, to discuss radio transmissions. He had never met Igor, the clandestine radio operator.

"Good morning. May I ask who you are? I am looking for Jan Brouwers."

"Good morning. I am a friend of Jan's. He is away on a coach trip to Folkestone, but will be back this evening. I am keeping an eye on the house while he is away."

"I see. Did Jan mention anything about a visit by the Gendarmerie, at any time?"

"Not that I know of. I believe that you are his landlord; is that right?"

"Yes, that is the case. Tell me, what are you doing in Mechelen?" Johan was becoming interested in the pronounced foreign accent Igor was displaying.

"I am here on a visit from Russia, to study city planning in Mechelen. You have a tremendous reputation for urban planning, and we are still rebuilding our cities, and modernising them, as I expect you know." Igor was playing for time, and waiting for the next difficult question.

"So how long will you be staying here?"

"Only a few days. My team has finished its work, and is waiting for instructions to return home. Jan and I met at the information office at the Grote Markt, and he offered to show me round the city."

"I see. Well perhaps you will ask Jan to give me a call when he returns. I must be going now." With that, Johan went out of the door, wondering how much importance to place on the presence of a third lodger. He would definitely ask Jan why he had let someone stay like this: it was not part of the arrangement to let anyone else, other than Anton, his coach driver, live there.

Flying through the tunnel in the darkness, illuminated by flashes of light every 375 metres as the train passed the connecting cross-tunnels, the six plotters settled down to their short journey under the sea.

"Security was tight, Galina, was it not? Can you see any weakness there?" asked Alain, the leader of the Spetnatz team, a man of few words, some unprintable. He was becoming more voluble now, under the influence of the experience of travelling through this technical marvel, on a train that was so swift and clean. "We cannot really tell what happens to the big lorries, can we? They have their separate route through the terminal, obviously. We will never see that, I suppose."

Galina spoke doubtfully. "The drivers have a special coach set behind the engine, at the front of the train, apparently, so they cannot do anything except sit in their coach during the journey. Apart from the weapons the guards are carrying, I think there would be no problems once you are actually inside the tunnel."

"That may be true, Galina, but our problem will be getting past the searches on the lorry route. It is sure to be a different matter when you arrive with a load of cargo. I understand they blow up suspect vehicles, rather than waste time searching. That would achieve nothing, and the tunnel would remain intact, while we would disappear without trace." Alain permitted himself a wide, toothy smile, like a jazz player between puffs on his trombone.

"That is not quite what we want, is it Alain? But have you not considered that if the bomb goes off inside the tunnel, far more people will be killed. Isn't that what you are planning?" Galina asked.

"That may be unfortunate but necessary. But the question

remains; if we put the bomb on a lorry, how do we escape the searches?"

"Alain, let us look at the security again when we come back. Perhaps we could make a mistake and go into the route reserved for lorries. As both terminals are identical in layout, we could have another look when we reach Folkestone."

Soon the train emerged into the blinding English light, and stopped silently at the unloading platform. Within minutes the Pegasus coach was waved on its way out of the Folkestone terminal, and turned right for Dover.

The visit to the town had a dramatic effect on Jan and Galina, and to a lesser extent on the Spetznatz team. They had been told over and over again that the British mainland did not suffer greatly during the war, by comparison with Russia, yet here they could see the huge extent of the damage caused by the heavy Luftwaffe raids, which could be seen on many buildings all these years later. The town was still not completely restored, but the massive castle - which had withstood the assaults of the French, Spanish and Dutch fleets, and had been the scene of so much activity at the time of the British evacuation from France in 1940 - was largely unscathed. The tour guide explained why: apparently Adolf Hitler had decided to have his first meal on English soil at Dover castle, to prove that he had exceeded all previous attempts to capture or destroy it. So it was that the Luftwaffe, and also the long range gun batteries which the Germans had deployed to shell Dover every week - to remind the inhabitants of their effortless superiority in artillery - were strictly forbidden to attack the castle. But the destruction caused by the V1 flying bombs, which arrived almost daily as the war neared its end, gave added evidence of the enormous devastation caused to the town and its inhabitants.

After a brief cafeteria meal in the ultra-modern terminal restaurant, it was time for the coach to make its return journey through the tunnel. As the Pegasus coach moved slowly through the twists and turns of the terminal approaches, patrolled by guides with radio handsets, Galina decided it would be too dangerous for the mission if they tried to go into the heavy goods vehicle route, and would draw attention to the bogus tourists at the back of the coach - even if Anton agreed to make the attempt. So they continued to the loading ramps.

On the way, Jan whispered to the Spetznatz team leader: "Alain, I hope you are studying this carefully, as both terminals are the same." Alain nodded, and was riveted to the window of the coach, trying to find a point of weakness.

Unfortunately, Jan was wrong about the similarity between the two terminals. Although they were both designed to be the same, only the British facility had been altered after the I.R.A. sent their lorry bomb over from Ireland, and the heavy vehicle route was changed. It now led directly through the Terminator, where entire vehicles with their cargo could be blown up without compensation if the bills of lading were false, or any other serious irregularities were found, either at the ticket office, the X-ray machine or the spot check area. The new terminal layout, which was not undertaken at Coquelles, would have made an attack on the tunnel more difficult from the French side.

CHAPTER 11

In Southern Ireland

The KGB was still thorough when it came to planning. Not content with sending an SVR team to Mechelen, followed by a Spetznatz team to look at the channel tunnel, they had planned a visit to Ireland at an early stage, to consult with the IRA. Their previous advances had been welcome: some weapons and explosives had changed hands, and valuable information acquired. This had been achieved by means of the covert staff always deployed in support of the Russian Embassy in Dublin, but now the SVR wanted to talk to the IRA planners who had shipped a two ton bomb over to England, destined for the channel tunnel until it was found in a lorry park after disembarkation from the ferry. Victor Krasnov of the SVR was an obvious choice again, and was instructed to make the journey to Ireland. His reliability was beyond question, and his involvement with Operation Kingdom had already produced results.

The ferry from Holyhead to Dun Laoghaire was an exciting follow-on after the flight from Warsaw to Manchester. The fresh sea breeze came as a surprise as it pushed damp, cold air in from the Irish sea. The smell of salt water wafted over the railway station as Victor walked to the ferry in the early evening. A night-time rendezvous had been arranged with the Provos, to ensure that local surveillance was kept to a minimum.

The ferry 'Pride of Holyhead' was the old British Rail Sealink's latest vessel, with a plush saloon and cocktail bar soon proving a popular meeting point for the exchange of Irish blarney, and endless variations on the theme of 'There was an Englishman, an Irishman and a Scotsman ...'

Victor thought of having a meal, but after a few vodkas the ship started to pitch and roll, making cabin staff sway on their way to the dining tables, and the non-seaworthy Russian visitor forget all about eating. The ship ploughed its lonely furrow into the teeth of a westerly wind, the seas piling up and the rain starting to obscure the sea views from the portholes. Victor tried to doze on a couch, without much success.

A few hours later the motion stopped, and the ship cruised quietly into the picturesque harbour of Dun Laoghaire, south of the wide Dublin Bay. It was dark and Victor found himself hemmed in by disembarking passengers queuing for the sea door on the port side. He wondered whether his contact - Seamus Cahill - would be there to meet him as planned. He was to wear a large orange scarf and a dark raincoat - the former only to be displayed at the last moment. Victor was to wear a bright red jersey and a standard Russian trilby: an unusual sartorial combination, but easy to recognise.

Seamus was waiting for him, wearing his distinctive orange scarf, and Victor felt a surge of relief. His quite good command of English nearly escaped him as he challenged Seamus nervously: "Hello - are you meeting someone from the River Moskva?" The expected reply - "Welcome to the Emerald Isle" - was a great boost to his confidence, and he eagerly grasped his host's outstretched hand.

"Come with me, my friend," said Seamus, and led the way through the brief customs formalities to a waiting Mercedes. They climbed in, and were soon on the road out of Dun Laoghaire, and off along a gently winding road through the sullen, moonlit hills leading to County Wicklow.

Arriving after midnight, Seamus Cahill led his guest to the door of a modest cottage and ushered him inside. A second

Provo stood inside the door, alert and with a welcoming smile.

"Is this the man who arranges supplies at just the right time?" the Provo enquired.

"Victor, let me introduce Patrick O'Connel, one of our very best," said Seamus. The two men shook hands warmly, then Patrick indicated a table, and asked: "Did you manage a meal on the boat? Not many do."

"*Nyet*, my friend. You are right. The Irish sea stands on end today." Victor sat down heavily, exhausted by the long journey, which had been unexpected. He had been given little notice of his trip to foreign parts.

"Well, it just happens that we have a meal ready for you both."

Soon the three men were eating noisily.

"Is this what you call Irish stew?" asked Victor, forging his way hungrily through the large chunks of steaming lamb and root vegetables.

"I can see you are already familiar with our staple diet of sheep and more sheep," replied Seamus cheerily. He was relieved to find that the Russian spoke such good English, if heavily accented.

"In Russia, we eat this goulash all the time. In Moscow, the choice is not great. Like you, the food we have is simple but good. Tell me, what is the name of this village?"

"That we cannot say, because walls have ears in Ireland."

"My friend" - interrupted Victor - "they have more ears in Moscow, I can assure you."

"Anyway," said Seamus "you are now our honoured guest, in an ancient feudal village near Baltinglass in County Wicklow. It has one river, two village shops, three pubs if you count the one on the high road to nowhere, and four big farms. If you look out of the window when it gets light" - Seamus stood up to examine the rain drops rattling against the window with undiminished ferocity - "you will see nothing but fields, trees and hedges. So we are quite alone here, and we have to keep it that way. You see, Victor, this is where our friend Patrick planned the attack on the Channel tunnel. It did not succeed, but could easily have done so, I can assure you. The time may come again, but at present we may have to observe a cease-fire at any moment. Of course, a cease-fire would not be permanent - it would come and go, on our terms, to suit our needs. When we stop fighting, the British are delighted, but it gives us time to re-arm and reorganise ourselves. Now, what would you like to know?"

Victor addressed his remarks to Patrick, the bomb expert. "Perhaps you could start by telling me why your mission failed?"

Patrick was in no mood to mince words. "It failed because" - and his accent became thicker with a quiet anger, which he controlled in the end - "one of our people did not have his heart in the operation."

"How did that happen?" enquired Victor, looking for clues. "In our organisation we select our operators very carefully, and the penalty for failure is not very pleasant."

"I can assure you that the same applies in our organisation," replied Patrick grimly. "But in this case, maybe the operation was too difficult, or the British too well prepared, but anyway our driver allowed his vehicle to be stopped and searched too easily" - Seamus slapped the table and it shook. "That was a tragic mistake. It could have been avoided in so many ways - bribery, better planning, or more effort, but to destroy a complicated operation by incompetence like that was totally unforgivable. The man actually left his vehicle unattended, and ended up having to pay the price."

"So, you had intended to blow up the channel tunnel?"

"Precisely, my friend. That was the mission, and although our bomb might only have destroyed the portal if it had been timed correctly, it would have been sensational, even if the tunnel could have been repaired."

"That is not quite our intention," said Victor. "We are hoping for a more permanent result. The end of the link with Europe."

"I can believe that, but how do you plan to go about your operation?" enquired Patrick.

"The rules of our organisation do not allow me to tell you exactly how we will attack" said Victor, remembering that a cease-fire might loosen the tight security formerly taken for granted in dealings with the Provos.

"But we assume you will drive a load of explosives into the train, with a lorry. It would be searched and found quite easily, I am afraid. If you were thinking of using a more modern type of explosive, that might be different."

"Tell me, how could we avoid the security searches?" asked Victor. He was careful to avoid discussion of the type of explosive to be used.

"Well, if we were doing it again - which God forbid because we don't repeat failed operations, and the damage would be far too serious politically even for us to contemplate - I think the bomb would have to be disguised better. Something like barrels of beer would be hard to check out in a big consignment, especially in the dark."

Victor's eyes narrowed, and he tried to avoid showing any reaction to this promising idea. "Patrick, one thing that interests us now is how you set the fuses for your bombs. Unlike you, we have little experience of that."

"I can tell you," said Seamus across the table, "and you have put your finger on something there. We have had a lot of accidents - too many to think about. Whoever is going to set the fuse has to be brave or stupid, but the problem has always been that the majority of fuses are either unreliable or too complicated. We prefer the old clockwork mechanisms, as they are simple and safe. The new electronic ones can so easily blow up in your face, as we have found out to our cost:

105

they can be hard to programme or even to read, especially in the dark."

"The best way, without any question, is for someone to set the fuse a short time before the explosion, and then find a quick way of escaping," said Patrick, stating the obvious for the benefit of his visitor.

"But in a tunnel, that would be difficult, would it not?" asked Victor.

"There is always the service tunnel. The train could be stopped and the bomber would have to hijack a maintenance vehicle to get away, but it is possible."

"Is that what you had planned?" asked Victor.

"Something like that. But you need more than one plan, of course," said Seamus. "We had several up our sleeves, right to the bitter end. I suppose you will be operating from the French end. The two terminals are supposed to be exactly the same, and in normal circumstances we might be able to help you by blowing up the transformer station at Folkestone, or staging some sort of diversion, but if a cease-fire applies I'm afraid we couldn't help at all."

"I understand," said Victor, "but after sending all that Semtex explosive over here, maybe we could still ask you for something when the time comes. We have no timetable for our operation - it is just a plan. In the SVR nowadays we just make plans, and then more plans. No-one knows if they will be used this year, next year or ever. But we are hopeful about this one."

"Well, we will see what we can do if our ceasefire is off when you are ready to strike," said Seamus. "We use ceasefires as a bargaining counter - they go on and off like a bomb timer itself. So we have to be careful not to compromise our strategy by side-shows. Now tell me, how is life in Moscow these days?"

Victor tried to suppress a yawn - unsuccessfully. He had not managed to sleep on the boat, and he knew that Seamus was going to leave for Dun Laoghaire before dawn.

"It can be described as difficult, but improving," he replied. "The inflation has had a terrible effect on prices for everything, and we don't know how to stop it except by another revolution - that is quite possible, believe me, although we have a very strong President, who has been elected for a second term with a good majority."

"So the Government cannot stop the price rises - do you not have price controls?"

"No, no longer. That did not work. Now, we still have rationing, but the supplies are not plentiful, and no-one can afford to buy. Before, there were always shortages - except of course for the KGB, but everyone got something." He laughed uneasily, remembering the good old days, but realised that the conversation was going nowhere. The past was in the past, and of no interest to his hosts.

"Would you both allow me to have a little rest, and then we can talk a bit more later, on the way to the ferry?"

"By all means," said Seamus. "There is a bed in the room over there, across the hall. You have two hours before we need to leave. I think they will give you some breakfast on the boat, or at least you can buy something to eat. The wind seems to have dropped, so it should be a calm crossing this time. I will wake you up when we have to go."

When Victor was gone, Seamus and Patrick had a quick and furtive discussion.

"I don't think you should have offered to help the Russians, Seamus," said Patrick. "You know how deeply we have been penetrated by the British MI5, and the word will get back to London if we are not careful."

"That is why I am taking our friend back to his ferry at dawn," said Seamus. "But this Russian project could be quite interesting if we are still on a war footing. The only problem is, we would want the bomb to go off at the British end of the tunnel, not on French territory."

"That would be too difficult for them," said Patrick. "The fuse would have to be set by hand at the last moment, as I suggested. You should tell Victor that, before he boards his ferry."

"But that means someone would have to set the fuse when the lorry was loaded onto the shuttle, like we planned, and then get out of the train" said Seamus. "Or someone travelling in the shuttle could do it. Then he would have to find a way of making it stop somewhere, and getting out. That's the problem."

"Maybe I should explain that to our friend as we drive along the T42 trunk road to Dublin," continued Seamus. "And I will also remind him that any help from us would have to be cleared with High Command before we can agree to do anything."

"I don't see the plan really working," said Patrick, who had all the benefits of hindsight. His experience had to be taken much more seriously than anyone else's. "I have a better idea. You tell Victor that we have been thinking, and because of our difficulty in operating from so far away, we suggest that he should take out the French transformer at Calais himself, to stop the train. Tell him that's all we can recommend at the moment, as we're on the wrong side of the water."

"OK. Now I'm going to set my alarm clock and get a few minutes rest myself," said Seamus. "Thanks for your help, Patrick. Our Russian partners should be very pleased to get all that free advice from the horse's mouth. I will see you later for breakfast, and try not to disturb you when we go off."

As dawn broke, Seamus woke Victor quietly and took him outside to the car, then drove away into the pale light of an Irish dawn. When they reached the trunk road to Dublin he broke the news that there could not be any IRA involvement in the risky Russian plan.

Victor was quite conciliatory: after all, the Provos had just made the operational plan for him. "Tell me one more thing, Seamus. Does the French transformer feed the train as it leaves Calais?"

"That is how we understand it. And the British train going the other way - to the east in the northern tunnel - is fed from Folkestone. But we have been told that the power could be fed in to either tunnel in an emergency, from either transformer. You will have to check that yourself - it might be critical."

The car eventually arrived back at the picturesque harbour of Dun Laoghaire, which was lit up in a bright sunrise, and Seamus accompanied Victor to the crowded boarding area. "Well, cheers, Victor, and thanks for coming all this way to see us. It has been a short visit, but you can always keep in touch through our friendly agent - the Maid of Kent - if you need to. She will always act as a go-between when you need more advice."

"Yes, that has worked to our advantage in the past. Now Seamus, please accept the grateful thanks of our government for your help. I think I can see how the operation might succeed now. Let us hope we meet again soon - if you go to war again."

"Let's think about that later, Victor. We cannot promise to get involved, but at least you have our latest ideas now."

"We will make sure your efforts are rewarded when the time comes," Victor promised, although he had no power to promise anything. "Goodbye, Seamus, and the best of luck." With a cheery wave, Victor left Ireland to its problems. He had his own.

It seemed that the plan for Operation Kingdom had become his responsibility, as far as the SVR were concerned. He would be the scapegoat this time, not someone of his own choosing, so it had better work, or he would have some delicate explaining to do. He liked the Provo's suggestion, to conceal the weapon in beer kegs. The odds against it being discovered looked better now. The I.R.A.'s experience with timers was interesting, and his confidence was returning.

Victor's new plan, made as the ferry pushed its way over the quietly rolling waves to Holyhead, was simple on paper, whereas before it had been totally foolhardy. In fact it might actually work, he began to think - or so the ever-present glass of vodka on the table assured him, as the vessel brought him back to England, and a tiring return flight to Moscow.

CHAPTER 12

In Mechelen and London

Galina Svetlov's return to Moscow was greeted with relief. She came back with new and useful information about the tunnel, so that when the details were put together with Victor Krasnov's they provided a complete blueprint for an attack - if it needed to be launched. The Defence Committee had not scheduled the subject for review at its next monthly meeting, so there was time for the KGB to decide on a workable plan and put it through the inevitable paperchase required by all modern military organisations, the ponderous but logical circulation of secret minutes and position papers so beloved of politicians and even the modern KGB.

In London, MI5 had just heard from a mole that the IRA had talked to a foreign agent about their failed attack on the Channel tunnel. At the same time, Interpol had managed to connect the voice prints and photographs provided by MI6 after their Middelheim visit, though the results were still inconclusive.

The outlook for the plotters at Donkerlei had taken a sudden turn for the worse, but they had already suffered a loss of status as a result of the SVR-Spetznatz visit, and the need for an SVR presence in Mechelen was no longer considered essential by the KGB. Spetznatz operations were now to be shifted to Calais, and reasons found to phase out the Mechelen connection which had achieved so little.

However there was still time for a farewell dinner in Mechelen, at which the original three plotters were to be entertained at the floating Greek restaurant on the River Dijle - the Kyrenia, near the Fish Market - sponsored by the indefatigable Galina, who had been sent back again from Moscow for the charade. It was her job to start folding up the Mechelen trio, but she never knew the details of the final send-off for each of the three men. She had been told that instructions would be sent to Donkerlei in a few days, and each would be told what he had to do.

Now, as each man walked towards the gang-plank leading up to the Kyrenia Restaurant, he wondered what would happen to him. The mission was virtually over unless the SVR or Spetznatz needed further help, but this was unlikely because a plan was just a plan, whereas security was a more important matter. Any word of the mission reaching the West spelled its doom.

Jan knew he could go to Waterloo if necessary, and hide for a time at his sister's house. Anton, as driver of the Pegasus coach, needed to remain in Mechelen, but unfortunately the Spetznatz knew how to find him at the coach stop in the Grote Markt. Igor was the most vulnerable of the trio. His job as radio operator was compromised, and his time had almost run out.

A cool mist swirled around the floating restaurant on the river Dijle as the quartet arrived at the ship. The nearby Fish Market added its quota of smells to the night air. The four climbed the sloping gangplank to the deck above, then turned left to the door of the restaurant. Inside, a warm and welcoming ambience with soft lighting awaited them as they stepped down the stairs.

They were shown to the first table on the right, reserved for late arrivals. The diners already seated appeared cheerful and contented, the waiters charming and attentive. The tables for four on either side of the central aisle, with pretty peach coloured tablecloths, made a comfortable picture of peace and serenity. It seemed like a perfect evening to the three SVR men. Galina told Jan what an excellent choice of venue he had made, and as he sat next to her and made social conversation the atmosphere was totally relaxed. He still wondered about their next role in Operation Kingdom, but this was no time to worry. He knew nothing of Galina's part in the evening's entertainment - he had merely made the reservation for the party.

The dinner went well at first. The Greek food was excellent, the ouzo and wine tasted better and better, so that by the time the last course was being served the party was in a mellow mood. Anton and Igor were on one side of the table, Jan and Galina on the other, their backs to the wall. They all failed to see a figure in a dark suit inching his way into the low-ceilinged and by now smoke-filled dining room, searching around for their table.

At first he did not find it, as it was behind him on the right. He turned, and then recognised Galina in the shadows by the wall. She froze as she realised that Alain had arrived to assassinate the Mechelen trio, not to parley with them. She had not been prepared for that, and hung on to Jan tightly, to protect him.

The other three had not seen the moving shadow fall across the table, and did not recognise Alain owing to the scarf around his face. The gunman turned towards the table menacingly. Galina nearly fainted, but managed to make eye contact with Alain, and nod her head towards Igor and Anton, sitting opposite her, like a judge pronouncing sentence.

As the gun was levelled there was absolute chaos. Diners shouted a warning to no avail. At first there was an audible click, and the intruder appeared to wrestle with his gun, then two shots rang out, and the smell of cordite filled the candle-lit room.

In the half-light it seemed that the only casualty was the remains of the Mousaka with vine leaves on the plates, and the honey balls just being served, as the two plotters singled out for execution dived out of sight below the solid oak table, and the waiter dropped four plates with a crash. The courageous Greek restaurant staff ran forward and tried to grab the assailant, but he dodged out of their way and ran up the stairs to the gang-plank in the uproar and confusion.

Very few diners saw Alain's face, but his voice sounded familiar to Jan as he shouted: "Keep still, this is a hold-up. Freeze!" In the semi-darkness and din only Galina knew how close she had been to losing her new friend if Alain had made a mistake, and how the blood which started to spurt from a waiter could have been Jan's. A ricochet off the table and the ship's side had found an innocent target.

The police arrived noisily in a few minutes, and questioned some of the diners by the entrance to the restaurant. Anton, Igor and Galina did their best to help, with Jan interpreting, and denied all knowledge of the assailant, so the police departed as quickly as they arrived, to pursue the would-be assassin.

Galina was as convincingly terrified as anyone. She did not really know if her own turn had come, and as she looked towards Alain's masked face she hoped that he was not a member of the infamous Volgograd Squad, known for their brutality and complete lack of concern for human life. In fact he was one of the outstanding members of that team, but in the close confines of the smoky dining room he had aimed only for Igor and Anton, and his Makarov automatic pistol had failed to fire, giving them time to escape under the table. The feather-light safety catch had moved during Alain's jump in the darkness, across the gang-plank and down the narrow stairs into the restaurant, so the Mechelen trio managed to survive that night by a stroke of luck.

The accidental movement of the safety catch was of

114

crucial importance to the Russian attack on the Channel Tunnel, and when the SVR in Moscow found out that Alain, alias Colonel Trimovich of the Spetznatz forces, had failed to carry out his mission, they redoubled their efforts to track down and destroy the Mechelen trio.

Galina, meanwhile, left for Moscow next day, expecting never to return. It seemed that her romance with Jan was over. The call of duty took its toll of human happiness, as so often happens, and Jan remained in ignorance of her complicity in the execution plan that so nearly succeeded.

In London, other matters were occupying the Northwest Europe section of MI6 dealing with the Middelheim meeting and subsequent car chase. A further call to Chuck Waters at the Nato listening station produced a disappointing result for Allan Gunn at Floor 14. No more transmissions had been heard from Mechelen, so no further information was passed to the police at Mechelen, the French DST or Interpol. Allan contemplated visiting the Moonshine station on his next visit to France and Belgium - it was just over the Belgian border in northwest Germany, and had the latest voice identification technology. He still wanted to match up the original radio transmissions with the recordings he took at Middelheim. This had still not been done.

Chuck Waters was encouraging. He returned Allan's phone call promptly and suggested a meeting the following week. "And another thing Allan, there will be a Nato meeting next week. They'll be discussing this thing, of course. You know how they're always stressing out those reinforcement plans - there just aren't enough troops over here these days, I guess. So we better come up with the latest hot gospel if we can. And hey, when am I coming to London? Remember what you promised me?"

"Hang in there Chuck," Allan replied in his best transatlantic manner. "You know me well enough - a man who always keeps his word. But just now we are stymied. There is a hunt for this Russian and Belgian team, the voice prints and photos I told you about are still with Interpol, and everyone is dragging their feet. They don't believe there's any problem, but I'm sure there is. Something in my bones says it may be a big one if we don't keep working on it."

"OK Allan, I guess my nose knows you are right. I'll look forward to seeing you next week; I am ready any time. Now, have a good one."

Allan was not at all sure about that. His next appointment was with the Minister, Ivor Jones, and the Controller West. It was a special meeting at the Department of Transport, called by the Minister to discuss what had become the latest hot topic - security in the tunnel - as long as the Government did not have to pick up the tab.

The Minister knew perfectly well by now that the Defence budget was ready to provide a paltry two million pounds and the Contingency fund, set aside to fill gaps in the budget or to fund the unexpected, a similar amount if it was matched by Paris. These amounts were totally inadequate, but in such a way did important affairs drag along, bringing tranquil days to the Ministerial staff and avoiding any semblance of stress to their abstract decision-making processes. The Permanent Under Secretary liked to keep it that way, so that he could keep juggling the balls, but no-one could catch them unless they were a career civil servant with at least twenty-five years' service, by which time they had either resigned, or resigned themselves to their boring daily round. The Association of First Division civil servants would take care of their pensions, and their ball-juggling days would be rewarded with a quiet and even more boring retirement.

The ministerial meeting was typically brief, and as ineffective as many others had been before. The funds were available but deliberately inadequate, the collective will was not willing on the other side of the Channel, and the proposed

Project Brunel equipment, which in the case of the American locomotive had been designed but not yet produced or tested, was still not available anyway. The key ingredient, as the Minister's staff constantly repeated like a mantra, was a huge central computer. This would over-ride the two separate computers which currently controlled train and passenger movements between Folkestone and Calais. The current equipment had been designed many years before, and it certainly worked, but it offered almost no automatic surveillance capability, and no chance of an orderly transfer of all the manifold control functions from one terminal to the other. That transfer would require at least the power of the latest Cray super-computer, which was so far officially in use only in the CIA and State Department in the USA, Nato headquarters and its listening station, and the European Union central statistical office. Others were employed clandestinely at NORAD in Cheyenne Mountain near Denver, and the National Security Administration at Fort Meade, Maryland. Then there were a few others which had been financed with oil money, drug receipts, extortion and other rackets in several third world countries which verged on starvation but required a close watch to be kept on their citizens, or regular updates on the production and prices of oil, gold and other marketable resources around the world.

The Channel Tunnel builders, Transmanche-Link, had never been able to afford a huge central computer operating both terminals simultaneously, and so two separate control systems, which were intrinsically incompatible, were installed. The hardware and also software on opposite sides of the waterway were not capable of cooperation, as they had escaped the common design principle which had otherwise dominated the project of the century, owing to the unending rivalry between the world's computer industries. The two separate tenders for the computer terminals had resulted in the clearly fair but unworkable result, that two companies were selected to provide two different computer control systems. Thus it was that the entire tunnel and rail traffic in it had to be controlled from Folkestone, because a handover was too difficult, and joint control out of the question.

The press and media very soon picked upon the weakness, which had been brought to light at the Department of Transport, and headlines appeared on front pages with derogatory articles by self-styled confidantes of the tunnel operators, who had become privy to the hitherto well-kept secrets of the enterprise. *The Times* of London, foreign owned and unfriendly to the Government of the U.K. said it all:

CHANNEL TUNNEL IS UNSAFE

The influential Parliamentary Transport Committee, taking its cue from evidence given to it by the Department of Transport, yesterday revealed that the Channel Tunnel is fundamentally unsafe owing to a computer mis-match between the British and French control systems. This design flaw, caused by different hardware and incompatible software systems in use at the two terminals, brings the possibility of a disaster akin to the sinking of the Titanic in its wake. With eight hundred passengers travelling in one Eurostar express, there is an obvious risk that a fire on board the train, however caused, could end up in a tragedy such as was last seen at Cannon Street underground station, when passengers were asphyxiated long before help could reach them.

The lack of an integrated control system to pass over the hundreds of functions from Folkestone - the main control station - to Calais means that a train stopped a few kilometres from Calais with a serious fire cannot be dealt with unless the British terminal's computer systems are used. This restricts the amount of help available from the French side of the Channel, which is not in control until a full handover takes place. On current estimates, the time taken to download computer information from Folkestone to Calais, followed by a transfer of full control, is believed to take anything up to half an hour 'on a good day', our transport correspondent was informed by a senior technician at the Folkestone terminal.

Needless to say, the informant asked for his name to be kept a closely guarded secret. 'It's more than my job's worth if this gets out', he volunteered. Bearing in mind the number of fires already suffered by trains using the tunnel, and the number of passengers carried through the tunnel today, the question must be when, not if, a dramatic incident will make the Cannon Street disaster look like a minor accident.

At Donkerlei the Mechelen trio settled down to a solemn discussion. Galina had left without further explanation of when she or Victor were likely to be in touch, and had said that the Spetznatz trio would be operating from Calais in future, owing to the problems of security at Mechelen. The three plotters at Donkerlei were to be congratulated on a most effective mission, and fresh orders would be despatched within a few days. Meanwhile they could have a short holiday, but should not leave the Mechelen area in case Moscow wanted to contact them. Igor was needed back in Moscow after that, with his Cyclox encoder and radio transmitter, and his return was a matter of the highest priority, although no date for his return was given.

Sitting around the kitchen table at Number 6, Jan took the lead in a rather tense conversation.

"You know, I smelled a rat in the Kyrenia restaurant. But the intruder seemed to be looking for money, and didn't mean to kill anyone - he just wanted to frighten them. What did he say? 'Keep still - this is a hold-up. Don't move'. He could hardly miss at that range."

Anton was less reassuring. "Suppose the intruder was sent to dispose of us," he suggested. "He seemed to know where we were sitting, and stopped at our table. I wouldn't put it past the SVR to arrange such a plan. What do you think, Igor?"

"I believe that is quite possible. We were given a warning by Galina that our job would be over now, and of course she would not have been informed of any plan to get rid of us - she seemed as frightened as we were when that lunatic started shooting. He obviously didn't intend to kill anyone, as he could hardly miss at that range, but why did he come to our table?"

"Because he couldn't see until he came under the lights by our table, the first on the right," said Jan. "You remember, it was much darker near the stairway, so he must have moved nearer the light so that he could be seen, but not too far inside the restaurant, so that he could get out quickly through the dark area near the stairs."

"Unless it was an assassination attempt," said Anton. "If it was, I am surprised that we are still here. After all, the SVR employs some of the best gunmen in Europe, and they normally use silenced weapons, don't they? This man had an ordinary automatic pistol."

"But Galina was a bit slow to react," said Igor. "I was sitting opposite her, and she hardly moved when the gunman stopped by our table."

"I think she was shocked and frightened like the rest of us," said Jan gallantly. "I wasn't looking at her because I was sitting beside her, and couldn't take my eyes off the intruder. I could hardly believe what I saw."

"Well, I suppose our mission is over anyway," said Igor. "I would like to think that the SVR could tell us what our next assignment will be, if this one is finished."

"That's why we've been asked to stay here," said Jan. "But have you ever thought that you, and we, are expendable? So if our mission is finished, either we go back to Moscow - except me of course, as I will continue to live here - or they find us a new job. They realise that Anton works for Pegasus Travel, and I think they would want him to continue, particularly now that Pegasus has started trips to England. Maybe Galina could have been more specific about the SVR's plans for us - unless she was not informed."

"If you ask me," said Anton seriously, "I think we are in danger of being sacrificed to the cause. You know how they operate. Galina would not be told - in fact she knows too much already and could be in a difficult position herself. I expect that was why she was made to go straight back to Moscow, with no authority to give us any more instructions."

"If that is so," said Igor, as if truth was suddenly dawning but he could not quite believe it, "we have helped to set this operation up, and it may never actually happen, but our lives are expendable. In fact if we are not needed the SVR might well want to take steps to dispose of us."

"Are you suggesting," said Jan, "that we may have to leave this house to avoid an unfriendly visit from our new partners in the Spetznatz? So where does that leave us with our landlord, Johan Diedericks? And how do we explain it to him?"

"I feel we should stay here until we receive fresh instructions," said Anton. "We should soon know the answer to those questions. Meanwhile, we should do what Galina suggested, and take a holiday here. I will continue to drive the coach, but not too far. Perhaps a short journey to Bruges, or Dinant on the Meuse - a favourite spot for tourists because they can imagine the filthy Boche crossing the river there in 1940 while they pour the good wine of the country down their parched throats."

"Maybe." Jan tried to be decisive. "But we have a moral

question here. Are you two going back to Moscow voluntarily now, leaving the project as it stands - ready to succeed but only a paper plan? Do you feel that it is safe to leave matters in the soiled hands of our friends in the Spetznatz to decide what happens? Or, do you think that the operation needs to be looked at again as a moral question? In the name of history, progress and humanity, do we still agree with the idea of helping a handful of the Old Guard to start another war in Europe?"

There was a silence, then Anton spoke. "If you are against that, Jan, then so am I. Igor, how do you see it?"

"I agree with you both. We should stay here and try to fight for the new democracy. I have suffered enough for ideology. You can't eat it, but it can eat you."

The three men were united at last in their lonely stand against a tyranny that was starting to take over and threaten their very lives.

CHAPTER 13

In Mechelen

Unknown to the Mechelen SVR trio, the Spetznatz team was now based in Calais, staying incognito at the Hotel des Bains, a short walk from the sand dunes on a deserted stretch of coastline. They had never left the area because the timetable was impossibly tight: to produce a workable plan in less than two weeks, but also carry out the other task - to eliminate the Mechelen plotters for the sake of security. The plan called for another visit to Donkerlei, to offer the occupants a part in the plan, then systematically murder all three using silenced pistols, and to depart quickly and quietly with the Cyclox encoder and transmitter.

The idea of using the Pegasus coach as a diversion had been considered by Victor Krasnov. The bomb would be placed on a truck, but a diversion using the coach would draw attention away from the real threat. But, as an influential member argued at the latest Spetznatz planning conference: Why use a complicated plan, using the discredited Mechelen team? They could cause the whole mission to fail, and anyway they could never be kept in place while the big wheels turned at the Defence Council. That might take months, and security at Mechelen was already compromised. No, the Mechelen trio had to go - but the manner of their departure would have to be planned as carefully as the main operation. This might appear difficult, but not impossible for a Spetznatz officer whose credentials included the coveted prize for marksmanship at the Volgograd Academy - of dirty tricks - and an unequalled reputation for thuggery and violence. During his last mission in Afghanistan he had captured three rebels, strung them upside down in their own headquarters, and after interrogation had set fire to the building, burning them alive.

Alain took it upon himself to hunt down the occupants at Donkerlei, with the other two as backup. He proposed to go disguised as a gendarme, or if no uniform could be found then as a long lost brother of Igor's - which the other two would not know about as long as Igor was the first to die. Not a pretty plan, but fairly simple to execute. A knock on the door after midnight with an excuse about security requiring an untimely visit, a discussion about the new Spetznatz plan needing two attack vehicles, the request for a cup of coffee, the sudden shooting. It was simple because anyone attempting to leave in a hurry would be intercepted by the other two men waiting outside - the normal Spetznatz routine. Then a quick trip to the river Dijle, a boat hired for the occasion, and three watery burials at night. Alternatively a visit to a nearby forest and a quick burial the same night. The plan only lacked one ingredient - surprise. If the occupants were at all prepared to defend themselves, and did not open the door - or if they had not been fooled by the bungled execution at the Kyrenia restaurant - surprise would be lost and the Spetznatz operators would have to break down the door. That could attract the neighbours' attention, and lead to another botched plan.

The French DST had by now been alerted to the presence on Belgian soil - with a possible mission at Calais - of a professional team of gangsters who ought to be followed up. The Mafia was the first suspect, but it seemed obvious that they did not need to rob a bank, as they could finance most European banks themselves. The possibility had occurred to the DST, and was endorsed by their new representative at the Calais terminal, that there could be a more sinister purpose to explain the appearance of sophisticated plotters in Belgium with Russian connections, using high frequency radio transmissions to Moscow. A trawl round the hotels of Calais, which Phillipe Villeneuve of the DST started on his own initiative, revealed that three athletic men with closely shaven heads had booked into a quiet, rather sleazy hotel near the seafront, and appeared set for a long stay - a suspicious activity in winter. A small group of DST operatives, masquerading as ladies of the night, was directed to look over the various hotels and find out, through their extensive grapevine, if any foreign visitors had descended upon the orderly local game of gamine and guy, which was practised so routinely at the world's seaports. The search was eagerly followed by male DST operators as well: volunteers were always forthcoming, and the assignment appealed as an excellent way of warming up an otherwise dull winter's investigative work. Some luxury, and even intimate hospitality, beckoned.

The attack on Number 6 was anticipated by Jan, and also Igor, who was especially vulnerable now. Their plan was to strengthen security at the front door, make prior contact with the formerly dangerous gendarmes, devise a rota system to defend the house, and to arrange a good escape route. Each man had a gun, and was trained to use it, but they did not possess the element of surprise. However a rear kitchen door gave them access to the small walled garden behind the house, and this led through a wicket gate to a large area of common land facing the huge old artillery barracks, which had just been knocked down to build a new Ministry of Finance headquarters. The dense ground cover of shrubs and grass provided an ideal place to hide if escape proved necessary.

Jan Brouwers personally favoured moving out of

Donkerlei, rather than risk confrontation, but the suspicions were after all only theories, and might be unfounded. Any move would have to be explained to Johan Diedericks with a plausible and well constructed story, but the idea appealed because Johan had another house in Mechelen, conveniently near the city centre, which would be more secure. Unfortunately matters could not wait any longer, as Alain's Spetznatz team struck while the defenders were still arguing about the merits of leaving or staying.

About an hour after midnight a knock on the front door brought Igor to his feet. At such a time, what could that mean? Another visit by the gendarmes? He went to the door and switched on the outer light. He was right - a Gendarme stood outside, wearing a moustache. Igor opened the door.

"Good evening. I am looking for someone making illegal radio transmissions in this area. I believe you know about our previous visits here? May I come in?" Igor had little time or choice but to admit the visitor: the trio had not rehearsed this possibility. Luckily Anton arrived at his side, armed. The Gendarme also had a sidearm on view. His voice and appearance seemed familiar to Anton, in spite of the disguise.

"I am sorry, but we cannot see you until the morning. We know nothing about your radio signals. Please come back after nine tomorrow." Anton was glad to hear Jan coming downstairs.

"Can you not recognise me? It is Alain of the Spetznatz. I thought it best to come in a disguise in case the neighbours looked out - they would not worry about a gendarme on his lawful business." The explanation was not convincing.

"What are you doing here at this time of night?" Jan confronted Alain in the narrow hallway. A tempting target, Alain thought. He wavered for a moment, then realised Jan was also armed.

"You know that we cannot risk coming here in daylight, because of your security problems. So I have come to arrange

126

a meeting elsewhere."

"Where are you staying?" asked Jan, trying to pin Alain down.

"That I cannot say. We are in lodgings, not far away, where it is safer. May I come in?"

"Just a minute" - Jan smelled a rat again - "It is late. We will meet you at your lodgings tomorrow. Now, please leave us. We are tired." The three faced Alain, and he decided to let them have their way, as they were all armed, unless...

"My two friends are outside. They gave me a lift here. Can you let us have a cup of coffee? We will certainly look forward to a meeting tomorrow, and then we can discuss your part in the plan - as a decoy, that will be your role. The details can wait until tomorrow." Alain was still thinking of completing the operation now. He backed to the door, and looked out.

"It is rather wet outside," he said. The other two Spetznatz men were stationed on either side of Donkerlei, waiting for a signal or the expected escape attempt.

"I would prefer to see you tomorrow." Jan spoke decisively. "I made a phone call to the Gendarmerie when you arrived, to ask why they were sending people here at night, and they denied all knowledge. They will be here in a few moments, and will be interested in your disguise, I should think." Jan made sure that his 9 mm Browning was clearly visible as he fingered it, then gripped it firmly as if to emphasise his words. Alain wavered again. Many years had passed since his famous exploits.

"All right. Let us meet at the Horseshoe at 6 o'clock tomorrow evening, and then we can go on to our lodgings, but please bring the Cyclox coding machine and transmitter, or have them ready for collection. We have been asked to take them to another address for security." With that Alain turned and walked out of the door. Unfortunately he had wavered too long, and a pair of real gendarmes were standing outside in the darkness. They presented their identity cards, and asked Alain for his.

"I am from the Brussels office, on a special mission," replied Alain, ignoring the request. "Are you on this case too? I was told it is highly classified, and we have been ordered not to reveal our identity to anyone."

The senior gendarme spoke to Jan. "Do you know this man, M'sieur?"

"Certainly not," replied Jan, showing annoyance. He needed to get rid of Alain as quickly as possible.

"All right. But someone telephoned urgently and asked us to call. We shall of course need an explanation, so I will have to come inside and take statements from you all."

At that point Alain saw his opportunity, and walked calmly out of the front door, into the darkness.

Jan realised he had some explaining to do, but the departure of the false gendarme provided him with what he needed.

"We thought we were in danger. I must explain that we have seen a gang of three men in this very street on more than one occasion in the past. They looked like terrorists or burglars, and this time we decided to call you."

The gendarme stiffened. He had heard about terrorists operating in the area. "OK, then you will come to our headquarters at van Busleydenstraat and tell us more about it tomorrow..."

His words were interrupted by the sound of a car starting outside. The two gendarmes went outside quickly. They could see two men getting into a car. "Halt!" yelled the senior gendarme, but he had not been quick enough. The car screamed off, without lights. The gendarmes returned, and spoke to each other for a moment.

"You seem to have had a lucky escape, M'sieur." Jan and the others could hardly disagree. "As I was saying, you can make a full statement tomorrow, but let me use your phone please." The gendarme spoke briefly to his headquarters, asking them to track a car which had just driven off, but the moonlight in Donkerlei had not given them a clear view of the vehicle - it was a very dark lane at night. So the two gendarmes departed empty-handed, and another execution attempt had failed.

This failure was to change the Mechelen plotters' chances of survival, and their role in the Channel Tunnel plot. They were once again to be a possible ingredient of the action, if it ever took place. The Spetznatz team had to explain their failure to Moscow, but Alain was able to convince his Spetznatz masters, who relied entirely on his expert opinion, that they could keep their options open and either use the Mechelen trio or eliminate them later. They were, as Alain explained it, entirely unaware that their end had been very near. So it was that the Spetznatz headquarters instructed their operators in Calais to go ahead on this basis. The safety of the Mechelen trio was to be guaranteed for the moment, and cooperation resumed now that Pegasus Travel had started to make trips through the Tunnel. In this assessment, Galina Svetlov had assured the KGB that Jan Brouwers was reliable, and so his team, together with the alphabet men, were again regarded as comrades in arms. It was like a computer mismatch, and the old KGB would never have made such an unsound judgement at a crucial time for the Channel Tunnel project, or Operation Kingdom as it was now registered in their Cosmic Secret files.

CHAPTER 14

In Mechelen

In the morning, Jan and his friends had to make a statement to the Gendarmes at their headquarters not far from their house - in fact just across the river Dijle. They had rehearsed their parts, and managed to carry off the interview by leaving several matters in the air, while simulating general ignorance. They had called the Gendarmes because that was what gendarmes were for. The phantom radio signals were mentioned by the inspector, in an aside to test Jan's complicity or knowledge, but he simply maintained that there had been a group of men operating at night in the area, and it was a pity that the gendarmes, when summoned, had failed to arrest them. Anyone could make broadcasts from a van, and keep moving on. This let the Mechelen trio off the hook, and as Alain's getaway car had been dimly visible in the moonlight from their doorway in Donkerlei, another fruitless search would now be started. They were obviously not implicated any more.

Unknown to anyone outside MI6 and the DST in France, another high frequency broadcast had been picked up, emanating from Calais in Russian, *en clair*. The frequency used was very close to that intercepted before, and control seemed to have the same signing off mannerisms. After translation the brief exchange was recorded as:

Calais: We are now set up but need the equipment.

Control: Agreed. We will provide from local sources.
You have authority to collect.
Calais: Understood. We will act accordingly.

The messages ended abruptly, but the listening station in Northwest Germany had no difficulty in analysing the signal frequency and similarity between this and the previous coded transmissions, so a full time watch was placed on the Calais transmitter. Thus it was that a further message was picked up next day, the morning after the failed Spetznatz murder bid at Donkerlei:

Calais: We will have a joint meeting later today. Have you any special instructions.
Control: Yes. Please ensure both teams remain in being. No further action to reduce numbers.
Calais: Received and understood. Will report tomorrow.

By now the Moonshine listening station had compared frequency and direction of the two new sets of transmissions with the original signals from Belgium, and decided that they could be related. Chuck Waters came on the phone to Allan Gunn with dramatic news.

"Hey, how're you doing over there in the land of Shakespeare?"

"Fine, thanks, Moonshine. What's bugging you? We thought you were all on vacation, or honked off with the project we discussed last time."

"Well, I guess we have news from the horse's mouth, so to speak."

"Spill it, you old spy-catcher."

"We've just gotten some signals from Calais" - Chuck liked to pronounce it Cal-lay.

Allan listened intently.

"Are you there, Firearm?"

"I certainly am. Please do proceed, Chuck."

"OK. These signals tie up with the two we had last month from Belgium - or so our guys tell me. But they are kinda kooky. So we have around-the-clock surveillance, and feel we might be onta somethin'. You did say you thought that Cal-lay was involved, did you not?"

"We wouldn't be surprised. The results of our recent excursion to the capital of Europe made us think that Calais might be the objective."

"Jeez, well we'd better keep on listening here, huh? But remember, you guys are supposed to be pushing the boat out for us in old London town, right?"

"That's right on the button, Moonshine, but we'd better stick to our posts a bit longer in case you hear some more - don't you agree?"

"Yeah, I guess you're right. We'll hang in a bit longer and see if anything gives. But don't forget to keep things warm until we get there."

"You bet we will, Moonshine. Now, have a good one."

"Alrighty, Firearm. So long now."

Allan immediately contacted the DST in Paris, who spoke to their man in Calais. The search in Calais was placed on higher priority, and the Mechelen search given another badly needed shot in the arm. The net was closing, even if the targets were still elusive. It seemed only a matter of time if the pressure could be maintained. Allan Gunn was determined to press on, as usual.

Back in Mechelen, it was a dull winter's day. Jan Brouwers and 'Alain' were due to meet at 6 p.m. at the Horseshoe, and an argument started at Donkerlei over the question of who should go - all, or just Jan. Eventually it was decided they should all go, in case of further trouble, which seemed to be a constant feature of this mission. Jan took the precaution of booking a table in the back room - a small alcove off the main bar, but still within sight of the patron and his guests.

The trio arrived early, Jan hiding the 9 mm Browning under his coat - just in case - and they waited for the three Spetznatz men to arrive. To Jan's surprise, only Alain came in. The other two waited in a car outside, as before. This was a favourite Spetznatz manœuvre, to show weakness but keep a stronger backup force nearby. Luckily for Jan, Alain had received instructions to keep the Mechelen trio in on the act, so he told the backup force to keep out of the way initially, and await events.

"How did you get on with the Gendarmes this morning?" Alain asked when the two men were installed in the back alcove. His manner was friendly, in contrast to Jan's cool initial greeting.

"They wanted to know why I had called them," said Jan. "I explained that we were a bit nervous because when we were having dinner at a restaurant a few days ago, a man with a gun burst in and came to our table. Then he started shooting."

Jan paused to see if Alain would react. No reaction at all.

"The man shouted: 'Keep still. This is a holdup. Freeze.' What would you have said if you had been the intruder, Alain? Would you have used words like that? We still have no idea what the gunman was trying to achieve."

Alain avoided the bait easily, as he always did. His long training and experience put him a few dozen steps ahead of the rest of the field at this sort of talk.

"I would have said nothing, Jan. A voice is a complete give-away." His voice was so similar, Jan thought.

"I quite agree, Alain. The voice was very like yours, and spoke in English, which was strange. But there is something you should know - the Gendarmes saw the number plate on your car last night. They will be looking for it now. I hope you are not parked outside."

Alain stiffened, and appeared to want to end the discussion, but kept himself in check. "If they find my car, my men will keep them away, I can assure you. Now, I have come to tell you that Control wants us to operate together as a team. The plan is for the weapon to be on board a truck, but the Pegasus coach will be used to stage a diversion, as I was saying last night - it may be necessary to start a fire in it, and when that happens the truck will be waved forward and possibly avoid a proper security check. Will you be able to get permission to take the Pegasus coach through the tunnel again without attracting suspicion?"

"That might be risky," said Jan, "but Anton will try to find out and let you know tomorrow, or soon after."

"Good. Now I would like to talk to Jan for a few minutes," said Alain to the other two SVR men, who had not said a word so far. "Could you both go into the bar for a moment?" Anton and Igor did as they were asked with some reluctance, leaving Jan alone with the infamous Trimovich, who spoke to Jan briefly and sincerely now.

"Jan, you know how important this operation is. Do you think we can rely on the other two?" This was a favourite KGB approach to see if any doubt might be cast on anyone's loyalty. If it did, there would be a suspension of trust and dialogue until it was re-established by positive evidence of their reliability.

"Yes I think so, without question" Jan replied, realising how carefully Alain was listening to his reply.

"You see, it is vital that we have complete secrecy. Our mission, if approved, could change the course of history - for Europe and possibly the whole world." Alain's voice seemed to rise to a harsher pitch as he mouthed well-worn words that had been used by dictators in the past, and probably would be in the future.

"Tell me, Alain," enquired Jan quietly, "what really drives you about this mission?"

"It is a long story, Jan." Alain had calmed down again. "I have a pathological hatred for the German race - if that is a correct description for the mixture of sub-races they really are - and this is the only way left for those who survived the Great Patriotic War to get their just revenge."

"But you were too young to remember, were you not? You are younger than me, I am sure. It is our parents who suffered. And my two friends here also suffered that way."

"Jan, I can remember it only too well. My parents were farmers in the Ukraine, near Kiev. The Germans came to us one night, in the freezing rain, took over our house and farm to shelter their accursed Wehrmacht, and threw us all out in the mud, on our own land. We had to stay in a cowshed for several weeks to keep out of sight. We were nearly starving when they left in a hurry. But first they burnt down our house, and then came looking for my parents, who were hoping to occupy the house again. They killed them both. I was outside, looking for turnips for our evening meal, when the farmhouse went up in flames. I went back to the cowshed, and found my parents lying still, covered in blood on the filthy straw. I ran to a neighbour's house, and they took me in, but refused to visit my parents' house in case the Nazi murderers were still there, looking for more blood. So my parents died like that, on their own, and I was an orphan, to be brought up by strangers who did not want to care for me at all. I had to beg and steal to keep alive, and I do it still, I am afraid. The Army took me in as a cadet, so I could stop begging, but I will always steal. It is a habit."

Jan listened quietly, much moved.

"I too had a similar experience here in Belgium, which you may know if Galina has told you, but now I feel we must try to go forward, not back."

"You mistake me, Jan. I intend to go forwards, but this

135

time it will be in my own way. We are only here once, to play our small part. I intend to play my part, but it will not be a small one."

"I appreciate your feelings about the Patriotic War, although thank God it was a long time ago. I too can't forget what happened to my parents in a concentration camp. I would like to help you. Let us shake on that - to us!"

The two men shook hands, united by their grief. Alain was almost overcome with emotion at the thought of what he had nearly done to Jan. His memories of the war had kept coming back: the house a blazing ruin, his parents lying on the blood-soaked straw. That violence had made him what he had become. It was a most improbable reconciliation, the two men united by a common bond of sorrow after the loss of their parents, their youth and their hopes.

"I want you to realise, Jan," said Alain very precisely now, "that Galina Svetlov told me you are completely trustworthy - whatever that means in today's world - and that I should protect you. I will try to do that. But your two friends are, in my opinion, expendable when their work is done. They must either come back to Russia or face the consequences. The SVR has a very long arm. They cannot stay here as settlers or illegal immigrants. Do you not see that?"

"I will try to see that, Alain. But do me a small favour. I will not reveal it to the others, but what is your real name? I would just like to know - such things are important if we are to work together."

"I am really Colonel Trimovich, of the Russian Army, on loan to the Spetznatz special forces, and this is my last job before I retire to my beautiful Ukraine, which is no longer part of Russia. But my past belongs to the old Russia, which helped to make me into a man, not to this Western capitalist country that is being forced into an unreal existence. I would like the old Russia to return, so now do you see? I have one last chance to succeed, by using force if necessary - but that is how we are trained to operate in the Spetznatz forces."

The patron hovered nearby, pretending not to hear or to interrupt, but finding a lull in the conversation asked: "M'sieurs, your friends in the bar are asking, what will you have to drink? I think they are themselves quite full up already."

"That is a good idea. We were only talking business which does not concern them," said Jan. The patron was fascinated, as he had overheard quite a lot of the conversation, but did not understand it properly, as he only spoke Flemish. "Please ask them to join us in a few minutes for another round, at my expense. What will you have now?" he asked Alain.

"Mine will be a vodka - preferably large, with no water." He smiled at the patron, who smiled back. "Good, mine will be the same, please," said Jan. The patron's look spoke many words, but he obligingly disappeared, and returned shortly afterwards with two large, yellow-coloured vodkas on a silvery tray. "I have asked your friends to pay, as they themselves suggested it."

The two men drank to the future, not the past, and together they had the power to change it. But in the special forces, Russian, British, American and others, mutual trust was earned by actions not words, and lack of loyalty usually ended in savage retribution. Jan knew that well, and had to think about it many times during the coming days.

CHAPTER 15

At Calais

The events of the previous night, and the meeting with Jan Brouwers next day, did not prevent Alain from switching his mind back to the urgent call of duty. The Spetznatz men were cool and dedicated ruffians, and their true characters would never be revealed to the public, who would probably not like to know them. Dedication like theirs was inhuman, and almost super-human, but it existed among these specialists of the Russian army. The next move was up to them. They had to prove themselves every day after their failure to kill the Mechelen SVR spies. This had been forgiven, but not forgotten.

Another visit to the Calais terminal the following morning revealed a point of possible weakness: the French security staff were kept so busy that they might fail if presented with a serious overload. The Spetznatz team were discussing this in their room when a phone call came from the reception desk at the Hotel des Bains: could M'sieur Delbois please come to Reception?

"Certainly. Is there any problem?"

"Not at all. An official of the security services is checking out all the guests, that is all. I apologise but am sure there will be no problem for you."

Alain hesitated. "Good, I will be down in a few minutes." He put the phone down slowly.

The alphabet men had some thinking to do. Their military appearance and haircuts made them conspicuous, and their feeble attempts at speaking French did not help. An alias or explanation for the presence of three such men sharing a room at the hotel might be hard to find just now.

"Be careful - I will go down alone," said Alain. "You will either have to stay here but be ready to leave in a hurry, or take a quick walk along the plage." Alain waved towards the door - the fire escape was at the end of the corridor.

"You had better get out now, have a look round, and come back in an hour or so."

The two got up and left quietly by the door at the end of the passageway. The day looked like becoming a disaster for the Spetznatz team. Alain made a brief phone call to a nearby restaurant to reserve a table for the evening, then went down to the reception desk.

"Ah, M'sieur Delbois, I thank you for coming down." The concierge was polite and charming, as usual, in contrast to the rather derelict appearance of the hotel.

"Now, we 'ave this visit by the Securité - do you prefer that I speak French?

"English, please," said Alain. "I am not French."

"OK. Permit me to introduce Monsieur Bonchance, of the security service. All 'e wants to know is where you come from, why you stay 'ere, and to where you will depart."

Alain was pleased that his two close cropped operators had gone out.

"As you might expect, I am here on some business in the city. I cannot reveal the nature of it, of course - but you would not expect me to."

"Ah, bon, M'sieur Delbois, of course we do not expect that. The real question is, from where do you come, and to where are you departing?"

"I think you have that in your hotel register which I signed a few days ago."

"Ah yes, so we do 'ave it." The concierge looked through his register.

"Ere it is. It says you come from Bruxelles and will depart to Antwerpen on the 26th of this month. Is that what you are looking for, Monsieur Bonchance?"

"Yes, but my question is more simple. Although there is freedom of movement in the European Union, there are times when we ask: who is this person, and what are they doing here? I am sure you understand that must be our business, and the question is entirely a routine one, I can assure you."

"Of course," said Alain, "I understand that. I have come on business for a Belgian company in Brussels, and will be returning there tomorrow after a visit to Antwerp. Do you need any more information?"

"No, that will be alright, Monsieur Delbois," said the security man. "If we have to see you again, we know where to find you. Thank you for your help."

Alain was calm as ever. It seemed that the danger had passed.

"One last thing, Monsieur Delbois - can you tell me about your two friends. I believe they are sharing a suite with you?"

Alain was more or less ready for this.

"They are part of my sales force, and are not in at present, but if you want to see them I can arrange for them to be here - where will you be located, Inspector?"

"We come and go, but if I wish to see them I will speak to the management here. Thank you for your time."

With that the interview was over, but Alain could see, as he left the desk, that the security man insisted on taking away a copy of the guest register.

In Mechelen, the Gendarmes had received another prod, originating from the DST in France, requesting a further search for what had become known as the Mechelen Mafia. The Gendarmes sent to Donkerlei, and the whole array of streets to the north of the river Dijle, so near to their headquarters at van Busleydenstraat, had by now realised they were chasing a cold scent, so their visit was more symbolic than serious. No more signals had been received from the area, and the car they were looking for must obviously have been disposed of somewhere. The river Dijle was a popular resting place for cars which were no longer required by their users, legitimate or otherwise. However, although an enterprising Mechelen firm was regularly lifting these vehicles from the bottom of the river for scrap ('The vehicle will be sold if not claimed within one month', read their regular advertisement in the local paper), the odds of finding a particular car had proved to be like winning a lottery. So the search for the Mechelen Mafia was gradually wound down again.

In Calais Alain was now the unlucky operator of the secret transmitter with its Cyclox encoder, which he did not really understand, and the machine was stored in a wardrobe, set on general standby mode for signal or voice. Suddenly it bleeped. Alain picked up the earphones, cursing audibly, and heard the familiar voice of Victor Krasnov speaking in clear - a most unusual departure from security procedures.

"Is that Alain?"

"Yes. Please proceed." Those were the agreed passwords to guarantee that the listener was genuine.

"We have directions to go ahead with the plan. Do you follow?"

"Do you mean, to carry out the project?"

"Yes."

There was a hush, apart from the crackle of the faint radio background noise, then Alain spoke again, his voice betraying concern.

"If I hear you correctly, we have to get ready without delay. Can you give me any more information?"

"You will get that from a friend in Leuven, who can give you all the details. There is no need for me to continue now."

A cold panic gripped Alain. He realised he had been left holding the baby in the hot bathwater, but it was probably a baby nuclear weapon, which had not yet arrived but soon would.

"OK. When will we hear from your friend?"

"Within one or two days. He will pass on all the instructions you need. That is all now. Goodbye." With that, the otherwise clear call went dead, and an equally dead hand grasped Alain's stomach. The mission impossible was to be his now, and perhaps his alone. The penalty for another failure would also be his.

Alain did not know, of course, that the new hardline President of Russia, who came to power dramatically on the sudden death of the last incumbent, had decided to go ahead with the immensely risky project of severing the link between Britain and France, after only a few weeks in office. The KGB, at their first presidential briefing, had been instrumental in pushing for this absurdly dangerous scheme to go ahead, while there was a power vacuum elsewhere in Europe and America. At the last meeting of the Defence Council, a largely unknown staff officer had been led into the chamber and introduced as 'Our eyes and ears in Western Europe and Nato'.

He had galvanised the Council when he revealed that the Pentagon had made extensive preparations to reinforce the United Kingdom before any future war could start in Europe. A huge airfield had been built in Scotland, on a scale never seen before anywhere in the world, to allow large transport aircraft to fly in by day and night, landing four at a time, side by side on the vast runway. It would be possible to land elements of three operational divisions within 24 hours of the go-ahead. Then they would be sent through the Channel Tunnel and deployed with their stockpiled equipment, to protect vital mobilisation centres in France, Belgium and north Germany within two days of a Red Alert being called. This would affect the military balance in Europe, so that any surprise attack would be extremely unwise.

Alain was glad to see his two Spetznatz conspirators return safely later that day. He sat them down and spoke to them urgently.

"Please listen carefully. From now on, you are part of my sales team, and we work for a company in Brussels. That is what I have told the investigator who saw me this morning. My name is Delbois, and in case you are asked I suggest you use names beginning with E and F, then we will remember them: Engels and Fransen will do."

"Can you give us some more information, in case we are asked to account for our presence here?" said Bernard.

"Yes. Just say you are on export business and cannot reveal the details owing to professional secrecy and the problems of competition here: speak in English and ask them to refer to me for any more details. Now, listen carefully. I have just received a message from Control, to say that we must activate the mission. Victor Krasnov spoke directly to me by voice, and told me to get ready to carry out the operation. He did not give any more details, but said we would receive more information from an operator in Leuven. We may have to go into the tunnel at very short notice."

"We have been looking for a good place to hide, Alain." Bernard spoke as if he had guessed the outcome of the security check at the hotel already. As Alain's deputy, he had acted on his own initiative. A fair-haired, strongly built and tough fellow-Ukrainian, he was not a full-time careerist, but had been drafted into the Army in the days of the old Soviet Union, and had stayed to avoid a future of unemployment in the new Russia. He did not share Alain's extreme views, but looked up to him as a true professional and an inspiring leader.

"There is a deserted farmhouse in some fields which are

overgrown and neglected, about four miles to the west of Calais - very near to the Coquelles terminal. It could have been put there specially for us!"

Alain realised that a decision had already been made for them - they would be forced to leave the hotel soon, before any more questions revealed their true identity.

"Did anyone see you when you went to the farm, Bernard?"

"No. We walked down a track, and then went behind the farm buildings. The area is well hidden from the main road."

"How do you know it is not occupied?"

"It is completely boarded up for some reason. Perhaps the farmer died" - Alain listened, but could not help reflecting on his farming parents' fate in the distant past - "or perhaps the land has been set aside - have you heard about this crazy European idea of cutting down production but still paying farmers to produce nothing?"

Alain laughed for the second time in the mission. "Only in the West - and western Europe itself - could they think up such a stupid idea. The place sounds interesting. Well done, Bernard. But you will have to check it out again today, because we will have to leave this place. Do you think we could move in straight away?"

"If we are going to be interrogated here, I think we should go now." Charles spoke his mind in a decisive tone of voice. The three alphabet men tended to speak in alphabetical order, as it was their order of seniority. Charles was the junior member of the team, but no mean performer. He had been decorated for gallantry, and his energy had carried the day on many operations. A slightly thicker-set version of Bernard, the two could be mistaken for twins at first glance. "After all, good security men never give up. They are bound to come back and see who we are."

"I agree. They will want to eliminate all suspects at the hotel, and they have not yet done so," said Alain. Bernard nodded his agreement vigorously.

"Unless we go back to Mechelen," said Alain. "Anyway, we are expected to check out tomorrow. One of you must take a final look at the farm, and see if we could move in tomorrow. I may have to stay here to receive instructions."

"OK, I will go and have a second look at the place," said Bernard.

"Steady now," Alain countered. "Please remember what sort of operation this is. Very delicate, and it must be carried out perfectly. I will always remain in charge, and give the orders. Bernard, as second in command, your ideas are of course always welcome, but the responsibility will always fall on me to decide what we do."

"Alain, when are we expected to carry out the operation?" Bernard asked.

Charles added his thoughts before Alain could answer: "Yes, and how do we expect to get out of the tunnel when we have placed the bomb on board the train?"

"I am sure that Control is aware of the problems - they have had plenty of time to think about them." Alain had also begun to let doubt creep into his thinking, but not for long.

"We must trust this operator in Leuven to give us more facts. Until there is a workable plan we won't go without a direct order."

"I thought you said we have a direct order to carry out the mission," said Bernard, in even more doubt now.

"Yes, we have. Only the timings have not yet been decided," replied Alain, who was still wondering how to answer the question Charles had asked him.

"I hope that the reactions of the tunnel operators and their security staff have been taken into account," remarked Bernard, still not convinced that sufficient thought had gone into the planning.

"That is why we are going to use the other three - to provide a diversion, and give us a chance to escape," Alain

145

replied, although no such plan had yet been made. The idea of sacrificing the SVR trio was still perfectly acceptable to him: the fewer people alive after the bomb went off, the fewer difficulties would arise when the time came to deny Russian involvement. He kept these thoughts to himself for the moment.

"Now, let us try to make a final plan," said Alain to the other two. "I expect it to go like this. The bomb is delivered to us, and we are instructed how to use it. Then we inform Control briefly how the plan works, as they may decide against it. Then, we get the Mechelen people to come over here for my final briefing. By all means, interrupt me if you want to suggest anything different, or disagree."

There was silence, as the idea of the approaching Armageddon worked its way into the previously calm minds of the two men. They knew that Alain was retiring after the mission, to collect his pension, but they had other ideas of a more fulfilling life. "Then we arrange for the Pegasus coach to go ahead of us to the shuttle train. We follow it directly behind. The bomb will be in our truck, disguised. The coach is only needed to create a diversion - let us say it breaks down or catches fire, and to avoid us missing the shuttle we are waved through. Then the coach follows us later, but we all meet in the service wagon used by the drivers."

"Yes, OK so far. But how do we get out of the service wagon to arm the bomb?" asked Bernard.

"We have to stop the train, say at one of the crossover sections of the tunnel - or we have to arm the bomb before we go in."

A knock on the door brought the conversation to a sudden halt. Alain strode to the door, and wrenched it open. There was the security man, Monsieur Bonchance.

"I hope I am not disturbing you, Monsieur Delbois?"

Then the telephone rang noisily.

CHAPTER 16

At Calais

Alain had not expected the police to haunt him again so soon.

"Not at all" - he spoke briskly, even sharply, and too nervously. "But excuse me, Monsieur Bonchance, the phone is ringing and must be answered. I will see you in a minute."

He slammed the door rather too noisily in the Inspector's face. It locked automatically. Bernard snatched up the phone and listened. "It is someone from Leuven," he said.

"Get the number and say we will ring back shortly. Quickly!"

When that was over, Alain opened the door with a flourish, and Bonchance entered.

"Good day, once again, Monsieur Delbois. I see you have your two friends with you this time. Could we have a few words?"

"Certainly. I apologise for keeping you waiting." Alain turned to his two men.

"May I introduce Monsieur Bonchance, of the Securité? We have met before." The other two nodded warily.

"Enchanted," said the visitor. "It is just that I need to confirm some details of your friends' activities."

"Of course. These are my two business partners, Bernard and Charles. Please go ahead."

"I believe you said they are working in Bruxelles or Antwerp, or both?"

Alain looked down at the muddy shoes and distinctly nonbusiness attire worn by his co-plotters. "Yes. They have had a day off today. Tomorrow we go to Antwerp, on business."

"Are you checking out, then?"

"No, not yet. Tell me, why are you visiting this hotel?"

"We are looking for someone. I apologise, but to continue. Your reasons for staying here: do you come here often?"

"No, we were recommended to try this place by our company which is based in Latvia, at Riga, the capital. We are all in the engineering business."

"I see. That seems to be OK for the moment. But you realise that we may have to ask more questions later, if necessary?"

"Of course, we will be around, but I am afraid we will have to get on with our work now. We are rather busy at the moment. The export business is very difficult, you know, and we will have to see you later." With that, Alain indicated that the interview was over by walking to the door and opening it for the Inspector.

Bonchance left slowly and awkwardly, with a last minute wave of his hand. He had intended to stay longer, and find out more, but could see no reason to do so yet.

A silence descended on the three plotters after he had gone. Alain spoke in a more confident manner now, even if he did not feel it.

"That was good. I think they may not be really interested in us, but if he comes back again, make sure you are out." Alain pointed towards the fire escape on the landing with a stab of his forefinger. "Unfortunately, our time is running out, and we must say goodbye to the excellent cuisine here very soon, or suffer the consequences." The other two appreciated the joke - the food was terrible, and the clientèle sparse in consequence - an ideal choice of hotel, as it turned out. "You have the phone number we need to ring at Leuven, Bernard?"

"Yes, here it is. I suppose that must be the agent Victor mentioned. We can't meet him here, surely?"

"Certainly not, Bernard - that would be far too dangerous. We could meet at your deserted farm, I suppose, but perhaps it has no electric lights. Draw me a sketch of how to get to it, then I will make the phone call and describe it to our friend."

Charles, the artist of the trio, drew a sketch of the route from the hotel, and a rough drawing of the farmhouse, seen through a screen of trees.

"Good. Now I will ring our man from Leuven. It is mid-afternoon, so he could come today. We will see." Alain dialled the number.

A cultured voice answered: "This is Leuven 517219. Who is calling?"

Alain thought for a moment. "You telephoned this number twenty minutes ago. We are your friends." Another KGB idealogue - four words to confirm that it was safe to proceed. The Leuven agent spoke again.

"My name is Jensen. I would like to come and see you today, or tomorrow. Can you describe exactly where you are?"

Alain hesitated. He had made a booking at a restaurant to avoid being in the hotel for meals: they could have their first exploratory meeting there.

"You come into Calais on the E40, past Dunkerque still on the E40, then when you arrive at Calais you follow the coast road towards Wissant, on the D940. We will be at the Beau Geste restaurant, which is west of Calais, facing the sea, on the D940."

"I could make it by eight this evening - my car has seen better days. Who will I be looking for?"

"Give your name to the patron as Monsieur Olivier. He will expect you."

"And if he does not, who shall I ask for?"

"The name is Delbois."

"Expect me this evening, then." The line went dead.

Alain's reputation for ruthless efficiency was a little far-fetched, indeed it had been embellished by the Spetznatz to encourage the others, and it had begun to unravel as things got more complicated. He much preferred things to be simple, quick, and even bloodthirsty if the occasion demanded. Hence his reputation for ruthless deeds. He wondered what they could do at the restaurant, except eat. Too much talk would be dangerous, as the security forces seemed obsessed with finding him, and were getting much too close. The deserted farmhouse did not appeal, as Alain was getting hungry after several days spent avoiding the other guests at the hotel, and a grey sea mist with the feel of persistent drizzle had started to blow in from the sea. So much for sea bathing at the Hotel des Bains.

"Right, Bernard, go and see if this farmhouse is habitable in case we need it. Come back with an exact answer if possible - for one day, two days, one night, or two nights - or more. I will not tell the concierge we are checking out tomorrow, so if there is any doubt about your farm building, we will go to Mechelen for another discussion with this new agent - Jensen is his name."

"OK, boss." Bernard spoke more cheerfully now that things were starting to happen. "I can see you have everything under control. I will go now - and perhaps Charles can come with me. Then we can approach the farm from two directions - and avoid your constant visitor, Bonchance of the DST or whatever."

"Right, both of you go now. I will leave here by taxi at seven-thirty, so either come here or go directly to the Beau Geste - you had better find out where it is this afternoon, as it will be dark when you finish your task, I think."

The two men did not return to the hotel before Alain left, but before doing so he phoned the SVR trio at Mechelen to warn them that events were moving forwards very quickly, and they should be ready for anything. Jan Brouwers was at the end of the line.

"It is Alain here. Can we meet tomorrow, Jan? Is it safe to see you there?"

Jan hesitated, for good reasons. "Yes, I think it is, Alain. We seem to have escaped any further trouble from our friends in blue. When do you want to come?"

"I have to see some people this evening, then I will call you. I will come tomorrow, late morning. Perhaps we should meet at the Horseshoe at midday, or in the early afternoon."

"There is another place nearby, called the Maneblussers - the Moonrakers. I think that would be safer. It is in the next street - Canonstraat."

"Good, we will see you there tomorrow."

"On second thoughts, should we not meet in another part of the city, in case they are still looking for us. You never know. How about the Fish Market, where the Kyrenia floating restaurant is located. Do you know the area, Alain?"

"Yes, I think so." Alain had stupidly given himself away again. He had never had any time to get familiar with that area, except on one rather dramatic occasion.

Jan was quick to accommodate his nervous reply, which only confirmed that Alain had been the killer that night.

"Good. There is a large café called Den Anker there - the Anchor. I will arrange a quiet room for us. I will see you there from midday onwards, unless I hear from you again."

"Thank you, Jan. I will be there tomorrow. Goodbye."

Alain was beginning to regret his stupid mistake. Such things could be unfortunate.

CHAPTER 17

In Moscow

It came as a complete surprise when Galina Svetlov was sent for urgently by her boss, Victor Krasnov, in Moscow's KGB headquarters, to discuss Operation Kingdom. She thought that the plan had been filed. In truth, she would have preferred work to continue on it, as the occasional visit to Belgium had been like a breath of fresh air. She was beginning to think that no more holidays abroad would be on offer.

"Galina, we have a serious problem. I think that you can help, perhaps."

"You mean I have to go to Belgium again?" Galina was expecting it, half excited and half terrified of the project.

"Absolutely. There is no alternative. Let me explain very carefully. It is a most delicate matter."

Galina listened with interest, mixed with alarm at the recent turn of events which she already knew about.

"You see, Galina, these Mechelen people have made a big mistake."

"You mean, to have taken so long to prepare for the mission?"

"Not just that. Now we find - or I should say Trimovich of the Spetznatz has discovered - that we cannot accomplish the plan as intended. We now know that the SVR team cannot play their part in the operation, because" - he affected a theatrical disbelief and dismay - "apparently the Pegasus coach can not go on the same train as the truck carrying the bomb. Trucks go on a separate train, on their own. Coaches go on a different train, with the tourists and their cars. It is totally diabolical, is it not?"

"How do we know this for certain?"

"One of Trimovich's men asked at a ticket office, whether he could take a truck and a coach, and what the fares were. He was told they would have to travel at different times, on different trains. Nobody realised this before, and now we have to do something quickly - to make a new plan. There is no time to waste because the operation - and this is Cosmic Secret - has just been authorised by the new President."

"So you mean that we are in trouble also, Victor, because we failed to discover this problem before?"

"Precisely. Now we will have to find a solution which works, and very quickly indeed, or we may find that we are the ones with a problem. I am afraid you will have to go to Mechelen or Calais, meet these people and make a new plan which will work. It seems we don't need the coach at all, and so we cannot send the whole team through the tunnel."

"So we have to send half the number, in a truck - is that it?"

"Yes, that seems likely. But you must see how it can work. I was always concerned that we might not get the coach when we wanted it, anyway."

Galina thought for a moment, then said slowly: "So only three men can go. A driver, his assistant, and one other sitting in the middle of the cab. They could not carry more on the truck without attracting suspicion."

"That means that only the Spetznatz men are needed. The SVR would not be used. But could we rely on their silence?"

"I don't know, Victor." Galina hesitated momentarily. "But suppose they find out that Alain was meant to kill them on the riverboat restaurant, then we could not rely on them at all."

"And then," Victor said with rising concern in his voice,

"we would have to eliminate them properly this time - but of course, that would need authorisation again." It seemed just a practical detail to him.

Galina was not at all sure that she approved of the idea. Jan had become not only a new friend, but even a possible lifeline to the golden West of her dreams.

"I think we should instruct Jan Brouwers to go, as the man in the middle seat. He can be a sort of guide - after all we need a fluent speaker of Flemish and certainly French, with local knowledge which the Spetznatz don't have."

Victor's face lit up like a lighthouse. "That's it, Galina! You have it. I agree to that. Forget the Pegasus coach, and leave behind one of the Spetznatz men at Calais - he might be needed there, in case of any problems, as a sort of reserve and contact. The same with the SVR at Mechelen. The coach driver has to stay behind, of course, and the radio operator - he may need to take over the radio again. That means that Jan Brouwers should go."

"Fine, Victor. I will go to Mechelen first, and meet Jan, and unless he disagrees for a good reason I will instruct Alain to take him in the truck. I believe you have arranged for a truck to be provided for the operation?"

"Yes, we have an operator at Leuven who is doing this, and meeting Alain at Calais or somewhere. You will have to straighten out any problems when you go. I will get you on a flight to Brussels tomorrow, at the latest. The operation cannot wait any longer."

"OK Victor, I will go tomorrow. I prefer to go to Mechelen. Would you make sure that Jan Brouwers will be ready to collect me from Brussels airport, or meet me in Mechelen?"

"Yes Galya, have no fear, I will check that out now."

Only a few minutes later, Victor was back.

"You have to go to Mechelen, and see Alain near the Kyrenia floating restaurant, which you know so well. The meeting will be at another restaurant of course, in the Fish Market - the Vismarkt - called Den Anker, which means the anchor. But Jan Brouwers will collect you from Brussels airport first, when you arrive in the late morning. I will book a flight for you, making it an open return."

"Good. I think you are enjoying the thought that I will be meeting the assassin and his intended victim, Victor. But what if Jan finds out it was he?"

"I doubt if he will, but we must leave that to your good sense, to make a workable plan, and keep the two sides together for the moment."

"There is one other thing that troubles me, Victor. How do the three men get out of the tunnel alive?"

"That we will have to leave for Alain to work out," said Victor.

"But supposing he wants to get rid of the evidence? Then he will make sure there is only one survivor."

"If that is his intention, then his plan must be referred back to me for final authority, but it may well come to that."

"You know, Victor, we are not all born in Russia to die for Russia. Surely those days are over. We could have another life."

"You may be right, Galya, and perhaps that old way of thinking is the mistake which all our dictators have made in the past."

"Anyway, I will make sure the plan works," said Galina grimly. "You can rely on me to see to that." She was quite sure of herself now, for the first time. It would work, one way or the other.

Victor nodded. "I am sure you will succeed, Galya, as you have many times before. Good luck, and my best wishes." He was relieved that the blame would now fall on someone else. A full entry in his diary would take care of that small matter.

CHAPTER 18

At Mechelen

The plane was on time, and Jan Brouwers was delighted to see Galina Svetlov again. He embraced her enthusiastically.

"Now, what exactly brings you here, Galya? It must be the free capitalist air. You look marvellous!"

"Jan, this is a serious visit. Let us get into your car, and talk about it on the way."

There was no doubt that Galina was facing the hardest challenge of her life.

When they were out of the Brussels airport complex and on the E19 to Mechelen, they could talk properly about the dangerous mission which Jan no longer believed in. Even Galina was faltering, but resolute in her duty as a senior SVR official.

"Victor Krasnov has sent me to make the final plan for the mission, Jan. And I hope it works, for your sake." She put her hand on his knee, and Jan clasped it firmly.

"You sound rather dramatic, Galya, my dear. I hear that this plan is still very uncertain. Have you got the power to make it yourself?"

"Yes I have, this time. It will be a heavy responsibility, and I shall need your help, Jan."

"Of course, I will be most pleased to help. But your friend Alain seems not at all sure about what should be done next. He certainly hasn't confided in me."

"We will meet him in Mechelen - at the Fish Market. You remember that terrible evening well, I am sure. Then we can go over all the points together."

"I do remember that night only too well, Galya. I was more worried about you than anything else."

"And I was most worried about you," said Galina, with new-found concern. She felt even more sure now that Jan could be a heaven-sent passport to the West. But how?

"You said you were worried about me when we shared a bed," said Jan with feeling. "I do remember that," said Galina tenderly. Jan felt the response was genuine. "But here we are with a mission to complete," Jan went on, "and I know very little about it."

"All I can tell you now is that the operation has been given the green light," said Galina stoutly.

"But I have no idea how it will affect us here in Mechelen. The plan is quite beyond me now," complained Jan.

"We will discuss it thoroughly with Alain when we arrive. He is not allowed to go ahead without my authority, you will be glad to know." Galina seemed to be in charge with an amazing degree of freedom, unknown in the old KGB.

"But surely, you do not have this authority yourself? The KGB itself reports to the President."

"If the plan we make is the best that can be made, then I will have my authority - in fact I think they all want me to have the freedom to make mistakes - then they will be free of all blame if it fails. I shall have to spend a night and a day in Mechelen - is that safe now?"

"Oh yes, we have seen the last of the Gendarmes. We are on quite friendly terms now, although I would prefer not to visit their headquarters again. You know we had to go there after Alain came a few nights ago and we thought he was a Gendarme. I still wonder why he had to disguise himself."

Galina knew exactly why he had disguised himself, but could not reveal it. Any more revelations like that would blow up the whole operation, never mind the tunnel. She really wondered if the plot might have been better handled. Victor was past his best, and he was obviously looking forward to his retirement, like so many in the SVR these days. No risks would be taken, and incompetence was the result every time.

"Jan, the plan is roughly as follows." Galina spoke slowly, in something of a dream-like trance. Surely, the world could offer a better lifestyle than this, she fantasised. Yes, she assured herself, it could if the cards were played correctly, but the rules of the game kept on changing. "The mission has to go ahead now, but it will not be possible to take the Pegasus coach into the tunnel. It would go on a separate train anyway, and so it could play no part. Also, I believe we cannot rely on the coach. We have a truck arranged to load up barrels of lager beer at Leuven, and we propose to send you, together with Alain and his chosen team-mate, on the truck and into the tunnel. That is the final plan, except that you may well ask how we intend to destroy the tunnel and get out alive."

"I certainly would like to know how it can be done. Has that been decided?"

"Not yet. I am telling you all this before we meet Alain, because I am your friend and I don't want you to come to any harm. The truck will carry aluminium barrels which contain Stella Artois lager, except for one, which will contain the bomb."

"That sounds good, I can see it might work, but I am sure there will be a problem with the timer, and when it should be set. Alain did not seem to know how it should be done."

"It can either be set before the truck arrives in the tunnel, or by some other means while the vehicle is inside the tunnel: that is the part which needs more thought. We can discuss it with Alain, and reach an agreement."

"But suppose the truck or the train is delayed? Then the bomb will explode too early. Or, if everything goes on time,

158

then the bomb could explode at the other end, in England."

"We have this East German weapons expert coming to see us, to explain all the possibilities. His name is Dr Carl Jensen, and he will prepare the vehicle for its run to Calais, with its cargo."

"Why the East German connection?"

"Because," Galina spoke very quietly, as if to avoid being overheard, "they are still our friends, and have an interest in the mission."

"In the name of heaven, Galya, what is that supposed to mean?"

"There are thirty thousand nuclear weapons still missing in the old Soviet bloc, and the East Germans have hundreds of them. Also, many of them want the return of the old power blocs, not the new order. But that is a secret which you must guard closely, Jan, or your life will be in danger. Please promise me you will never reveal it to anyone."

"I promise. Don't worry about that." He gave her hand a squeeze, and decided not to argue any more, but to see how the mission could be made to fail.

"And please promise me never to reveal the source of the information. It is Cosmic Secret, like almost all our operational plans these days. Just let us pretend it is a matter of opinion, not fact. Is that clear?"

"Of course, I promise to keep it all to myself, on pain of death - yours and mine."

At last the N1 turnoff to Mechelen from the E19 came into view, and Jan drove up the Leopoldstraat towards the Vismarkt. Soon they passed through the Hoogstraat, then the Korenmarkt, and finally turned into the Vismarkt. Jan parked, with some foreboding, not far from the Kyrenia floating restaurant, and the two walked over to the Anker restaurant at the corner of a cobbled street. He motioned to Galina to enter first.

159

In the long bar on the right stood Alain, smiling, his hand outstretched to greet Galina. "Congratulations on finding us here. I had terrible trouble locating this place."

Jan could not resist mixed emotions at this obvious lie, but smiled at the sick joke.

"We had no problem at all, Alain," said Galina, playing for time. "Jan knows this area well, of course. I expect you heard about our experience in the Kyrenia restaurant, when the gunman came in and fired at a waiter?"

"Yes, you told me all about it. It must have been quite frightening when the gunman said 'freeze' and you all had to get under the table. I suppose the orange table-cloths must have hidden you quite well." Galina caught her breath. Alain was almost giving himself away again - what was his motive? Perhaps he didn't care any more.

"I remember telling you how we had to dive under the tables - luckily there was room for all of us, or the party might have ended differently," Galina volunteered. Then she switched from forced hilarity to her serious and rather earnest mode. "Now, let us see, where can we talk?"

Jan pointed towards a door at the end of the bar, and the trio entered a quiet back room, with four tables. They sat down heavily and expectantly. Alain spoke first.

"I came by train and left the other two in Calais. They don't need to know everything at this stage. Now, what can you tell us, Galina?" It was best to rely on her to fill in the details of the suicide mission.

"Alain, to start with, please tell me how your meeting went with Doctor Jensen yesterday."

"Fine. We had a good discussion about the use of beer barrels, as I am sure you know, and he has arranged for a vehicle to be loaded tomorrow, early in the morning."

"Good, that part is as we expected," said Galina. "But now he has to give you - and I would imagine Jan - some very careful instructions in the use of the special barrel and its equipment."

"Yes, we have arranged for that to be done this evening or early tomorrow morning. So will you be there, to make sure all is well, and to report back to Control?"

Galina nodded. "Yes, that is what I would like to do. But I will stay here tonight anyway. Now we have to look at the final plan. I believe that one of your men found that the Pegasus coach cannot accompany the truck?"

"I am afraid so. That does make it more difficult - we had planned to stage a diversion with the coach, so that the truck would be waved forward to catch the shuttle, then the coach would arrive behind it. But now we find that they would go on separate trains."

Galina spoke to Alain with authority now. "Control wants the truck to go on its own, with you, together with Jan as a guide, and one of your two men. The other should stay at Calais and report the situation either by telephone or radio. Are you clear about that?"

"If you say so. And if Jan feels he can carry out an active part in the mission. Things might turn nasty. There might even be some shooting."

Jan came into the conversation now. "I agree with Control. I believe the mission could fail unless someone can speak Flemish and French fluently. Did you not consider that?"

Alain seemed to agree reluctantly. "We did think about that, but it seemed a minor point."

Galina disagreed. "Alain, you do realise that if this mission fails, our heads will all roll. And had you not considered that the coach might not be available or ready on time? It might have missed the train anyway. I am beginning to wonder if you have made a proper plan for the operation."

"We have not had time yet - you know that perfectly well, Galina. Also, the police at Calais came to our hotel, looking for someone, and we had a job to convince them that we were not the people they were looking for."

161

"Now you see what I mean about the need for a French speaker, and a Flemish one, if you are coming from Leuven or Mechelen - they speak Flemish there." Galina was in full command now. "It really is time for you to get your act together, Alain."

"Well, we even thought of leaving the hotel immediately, to avoid any further questioning."

"Where did you plan to go to, then?"

"There is a deserted farmhouse nearby, but it has no lights, heat or telephone. I think we might be better off at another hotel, out of town preferably."

"Right, let us get down to business," Galina interrupted. Jan remained silent, watching these two making the absurd plan. "We can discuss your lodgings later. The next thing to do is meet Dr Jensen so that we can find out exactly how his device works. Have you thought about setting the timer?"

"Of course, Galina, but we need to see it first!"

At that moment the Patron came in. "Excuse me, but are you having anything to eat, or can I get you something to drink?"

"I wonder if you are staying open for another half hour?" Jan spoke perfect Flemish of course. "We have to make a phone call - would that be possible?".

"Certainly, and I can give you the account with your meal or drinks. I will show you where the phone is."

Galina came forward. "Jan, see how the phone works and then we will contact Jensen - we will do that together in case of a language problem." She spoke loudly, for Alain's benefit.

The phone call to Leuven was brief and luckily contact was made. A rendezvous in Brussels was decided upon, to avoid meeting at the agent's flat, which would have been risky.

"Now we can continue," Galina said. "We will meet Jensen tonight at an obvious place near the Grand Place in Brussels - Jan has told him to go to the Manneken Pis which is a well known landmark just off the Place - in the Rue du Midi - and then have our discussion in a room at the Novotel. Nobody will be watching us there - you just go in, collect a key, and take the elevator up to your room."

Alain spoke next. Jan was still leaving everything to Galina. "Galina, I don't know if you realise, but this is a kind of suicide mission." He paused for the obvious to sink in. The idea had certainly dawned at the KGB headquarters, and Jan's team also realised perfectly well that they might not survive if they took part. They had never expected to do so, and had regarded the whole operation as a plan to be filed away in the military archives. Under the rules of the new Russia, real warlike plans were almost forbidden, as the KGB had been penetrated by the CIA, and the lessons of 1941 - when they were urgently needed but had never been made - seemed to have been forgotten while the new detente with the West lasted. That was coming to a sad end.

Alain did not show any concern about the dangers of the mission. After all, in his experience Spetznatz men were usually the only survivors of any operation they took part in. Jan listened intently to Galina's reply.

"Alain, once again I have to ask you: what is your plan? You have been here for two weeks now, and Control is not at all pleased with the progress you have made. Now, please tell me how you see yourselves getting out of the tunnel alive." She shot a glance at Jan, who feigned a lack of concern which was wholly unwarranted. He wanted to come out alive, without the Spetznatz men.

"And have you discussed your plan with Jan here?" Jan shook his head briefly.

Alain replied defensively, aware that his professional competence was in question. "Galina, as I said, there has not been time to discuss the plan with Jan - you know how the Gendarmes made his house here in Mechelen completely unsafe for another visit, and we had to move elsewhere."

"Jan says it is safe now - for him at least, but probably not for you to visit - so I agree that you should not go back there. Now, assuming that you can set the timer on the bomb without difficulty, what is your plan?"

"We have discussed this at Calais, and my men were in agreement, but that was before we heard that the coach cannot come with us. We had planned either to set the timer before driving aboard the shuttle train, or if that proved impossible, or the time has to be changed, we planned to get the train to stop at an emergency platform in the tunnel. To do this we would start a fire in the drivers' coach. Then we could go back to our shuttle wagon, reset the timer, and get back into the coach. I admit that would be the tricky part. We might find the train guards would intervene, as they are always on hand in the train and the service tunnel."

"Well," said Galina, "that seems quite workable, until you look at the details. So it obviously needs more thinking. For a start, you haven't mentioned how you will get through the searches."

"Yes, we understand the searches are not too thorough," said Alain, "as long as the documents are in order. I suppose your German friend is handling the paperwork?"

"Those are his instructions. I believe it is quite normal to send supplies to the Folkestone terminal from France. They like French wine, and now we will say they have asked for Belgian lager. The paperwork is quite simple, I believe, for that sort of routine consignment."

"But can the bomb be detected? I believe there is a check on radio-activity?"

"I am assured that this weapon gives out practically no radio-activity. Also it will be shielded by all the other metal barrels, and the X-rays cannot penetrate them." Galina exuded a confidence which she certainly did not feel. "Now we will see how the meeting with Dr Jensen goes, before I approve the plan. But I will need to be convinced that you have thought of everything that can go wrong, and can explain to me how the three of you will get out alive. You do not seem to have considered that properly."

"There may have to be some sacrifices," Alain replied, his eyes resting briefly on Jan's solemn face.

CHAPTER 19

In Brussels

The meeting place by the Manneken Pis near the Grand Place was well chosen, and Dr Jensen arrived in good time, to the relief of Galina and the other two. The quartet moved on foot to the nearby Novotel, which Victor Krasnov had used when he visited the plotters a few weeks before. Galina had booked a room, and they were soon installed there.

Dr Jensen seemed charmingly efficient. His cover was as a chemical engineer for the Stella Artois brewery at Leuven, although he had nothing to prove the connection. It served him well, however, when he said he had worked with the rival Primus organisation at Haacht, but now wanted to export a truckload of Stella Artois lager to the channel tunnel terminal at Folkestone. The brewery, keen to cultivate such a prestigious outlet, had offered to provide the vehicle, as well as the very straightforward export papers. Payment was to be made after delivery - an event which was not likely, so the terms of business were ideal.

Dr Jensen started his presentation:

"Here I have a photograph of the timer for this weapon. Please watch carefully and make notes. Ask me any questions as you think of them - as many as possible please, and stop me if you do not understand.

"This timer can be set for up to 24 hours, but as you see, the dial is divided into half hour segments. This means that the timer cannot be set more accurately than about fifteen minutes, as the divisions are very small, so you cannot rely on an accuracy better than five minutes.

"When I have prepared the vehicle and its load, the special keg or barrel will be positioned out of sight, accessible if you know where to look. I will tell you how to find it at the end of this presentation. Any questions so far?"

Alain spoke first as usual.

"We have not yet told you where the vehicle should be delivered. May I confirm that now?"

"Certainly, and I will ask you for a sketch map of the place and how it can be approached, but I would prefer you to collect the vehicle from the Stella Artois brewery at Leuven if you can, otherwise I will be stranded at Calais."

"Good." Alain seemed quite satisfied. "You were very close to the place where we want the truck to go when you came to Calais last night. It is about five kilometres further down the D940, and then up a farm track to some woods near Wissant, where the German army had a huge launching site for their V2 rockets during the war. There is a deserted farmhouse up an earth track, and we want the vehicle to come to the back of the house. Then we could ask you any last minute questions. I can give you a sketch map, which we have prepared for you."

"Don't forget that the truck will be heavy, and may get stuck on bad roads, also I cannot agree a definite time for delivery until I have got a confirmed loading time at Leuven. I may have to ask you to collect, in order to make sure that the vehicle arrives safely. I am not supposed to take part in your operation, you see. Have you any other questions so far?"

Galina spoke next. "Are you saying that this timer" - she pointed at the photograph of the dial, which was about five centimetres wide - "can only be set once? Does it only go clockwise?"

"Yes. I am afraid it cannot go backwards. We had to provide a circular dial operated by clockwork, to conform to

167

the shape of the barrel, and make the timer easy to use. It cannot be changed to an earlier time, but it can be moved forwards, to give more time."

Jan spoke next, having been silent all this time, thinking about the enormity of the idea. It was a calculated affront to humanity to blow up several hundred passengers in a tunnel under the sea, worthy of any extreme terrorist organisation, such as had operated in Ireland, Britain, America, Spain, Lebanon, Gaza and Israel, to name a few. What was the point of all this mass killing, even if it was part of national policy? Who made these national policies, and who really wanted them? Nobody of course, unless they were either insane or were sycophantic politicians supporting a dictatorial government - which they always did. He decided that he was not mad, and would never agree to mass killing on this scale. "Can the timer be stopped, in case that is necessary?"

Alain looked at him, and then at Dr Jensen, as if it was an entirely superfluous question.

"I mean, we might not have reached the tunnel when the timer is set to go off." He was wondering if there was any way of stopping the enormous destruction, and perhaps getting out alive. Alain seemed not to have realised that his macho ideas were based on a history owing much to early Russian and Mongolian customs, when life itself was of no importance, and the dead were never counted. What was the point of counting the dead, when there were so many?

"No. I have already said that the only way to stop the timer from functioning is to wind it on, say to the 24 hour mark, and then make sure it is disconnected before the remaining time has elapsed."

"In that case, Alain, it is difficult to know how you should operate the timer."

Galina was getting worried, now that Jan was going to be a member of the suicide squad. She wondered why she had pressed for him to be included. A safe way out had to be part of the plan before she would agree to it.

"If this timer is so difficult to adjust, can we change it, or is it too late?" asked Galina.

"The normal electronic timer has a digital readout," said Dr Jensen, "but it is difficult to read in the dark, and very easy to get the time wrong. That is why we have given you a simple clockwork mechanism with a clear dial - you will find that simple things work better for everyone. Anyway, it is too late now to change to another device."

"We accept that," said Alain, "but there is another problem. We would prefer to set the dial before we go into the tunnel. But if the train is delayed, or the truck is held back to await the next train, we have to adjust the timer. So if we have already set it, and the truck is called forward, what do we do?"

"You will have to set the timer when the truck has been loaded onto the train," said Jensen. "Then, if you have set it to, let's say, an accuracy of fifteen minutes, there is no problem, assuming that the train takes thirty minutes to go through the tunnel."

"That makes sense," Alain said. "Now, tell us about the positioning of the special beer barrel."

"It will be placed near the centre of the load. We have to make it impossible to find by anyone briefly inspecting the load, so it will be one layer down in the stacks. So of course you do need to know exactly where it is, naturally."

"Is all this really necessary?" Galina was wondering how the timer could be re-adjusted in the heat of the moment, and probably in the dark.

"We have to keep the radio-activity out of the way of the sensors, which are used to check every goods vehicle for radio-activity. If they fail the search, we understand the vehicles may be blown up in a special enclosure," said Jan.

"That could be quite spectacular," said Jensen. "Although I am exaggerating, as a controlled explosion would not normally set off this type of bomb - it would just burn."

"Good. Now you will have to think again about getting out of the tunnel alive," said Galina. "It seems you must set the timer when you have driven into the train and are parked in the shuttle wagon. Then you will have to move the timer on again if the train is delayed. Perhaps you will have to leave your team-mate in the vehicle Alain, or stay there yourself?"

"If we could cut off the electric power, that would stop the train, would it not?" Alain was thinking aloud.

"In order to stop the train," said Jan, "according to our information there are only two methods, either to blow up a transformer - but it is too late to think of doing that now - or to make the driver stop the train."

"That would not be impossible," Alain replied. "The drivers of the goods vehicles are in a coach just behind the locomotive. So, if we could first get the train stopped by means of an emergency, such as a fire in the drivers' coach, we could get into the locomotive and make the driver stop it permanently, if all goes well. Let us say we might have to get rid of the drivers - there are two, are there not?"

"That sounds too easy, Alain. I am sure they have already thought of that. The train is under constant control from the terminals." Galina pressed on: "Have you considered anything else?"

Alain lied. "Not in detail. To get out alive we need two plans; one is to hijack the maintenance transport in the service tunnel, the other is to take over the train. But as you say, our informants tell us that it is controlled by computers in any emergency. So the second method may not work."

"I am afraid that you can only get out by the service tunnel," remarked Galina, stating the obvious - "unless you feel you can beat the train control system and cheat death itself into the bargain. So your plan must obviously include the takeover of one of the service vehicles - maintenance, fire or ambulance - to get out of the tunnel."

"Yes, I suppose so. Now, has anyone any more questions?" asked Dr Jensen. In truth, he did not want to be drawn into the complicated plan any more than he had been.

Surprisingly there were no more questions until Jan asked where the special barrel was going to be loaded.

"Of course, I had intended to make that the last question. The load will be ten barrels wide and twenty or so long - the exact numbers do not matter. Working from the front, position five ten means five to the right from the front, and ten to the rear. I will let you know exactly when the truck has been loaded. The barrel will be one layer down, so it will be out of sight. All this is most important, because if you cannot find the barrel when you need to, it means moving a large number before you find it."

"That seems very clear to me, Dr Jensen," said Galina. "I will not be there when the truck arrives, but Alain will probably collect it, and I am sure that we can trust you to carry out your part of the mission. Now we must let Alain get back to Calais, after he has given you the sketch of the farm location, in case it is needed. Alain, I think it would be best for me to stay here in Brussels, and for security reasons Jan too, until tomorrow. I expect the project to be authorised later this evening. So I want you to phone in every hour or so when you get back to Calais. Then I can give you instructions after Control has cleared our plan."

Galina continued: "Dr Jensen, I would like you to phone in here every two hours until midnight, and again from six in the morning, so that I can keep you informed, in case of any change of plan. Then I expect you to have the vehicle loaded early tomorrow morning, unless the plan changes. Have you any questions?"

"No thank you, Comrade Svetlov, my task is fairly simple, and I do not expect any problems. Good luck to you all."

"One final thought," Galina summed up: "Remember, this mission is not impossible - it will work if you have the right plan, which we have now. For security, in case we are overheard, if I say Status Red, that means the mission goes ahead tomorrow at the earliest opportunity, within eight hours. If I say Status Blue, the mission is postponed for eight hours, and you will need to have fresh instructions before you go ahead. If I say Status White, the mission is cancelled, but do not expect that."

When the other two had gone, Galina lay on a bed in the room at the Novotel, exhausted by the strain. She asked Jan to sit by her.

"Jan, I insist that you come out of this alive. Have you thought of that any more?"

"I am a hired hand, Galya, and I have to earn my living, possibly dangerously at times," Jan said tenderly. "If it were not for you, I am sure the KGB would have got rid of me a long time ago."

Galina thought, and then lied, not for the first time in her life as a secret agent. "Nonsense, Jan, the SVR needs you as a vital member of their team, and..." she put her arm round him and pulled him towards her on the bed, "I need you also, especially now. Together we can solve this problem. The world is in our hands," she said quietly. He lay beside her on the bed, then realised for the second time what a beautiful woman she was.

"Galya," he said, as he stroked her face, "I remember so well our last meeting at Mechelen, and how we enjoyed our night together. Can we do that once more? It may be the last time."

"You cannot go back to Mechelen tonight Jan. It is completely unsafe there, and I will not let you. If you stay with me, I am sure we can come to a conclusion about the mission and your part in it." Galina was beginning to think of it as hers now, to get a husband in the West and leave her native Russia for ever, as so many had done before. But everything still seemed uncertain. Then the two lovers lay back to enjoy the special KGB relationship, which to her was the best part of all the rule book's unwritten provisions.

"Tell me, Galya," Jan whispered, "why did you want me to go on this suicide mission. I could have survived in Mechelen."

"I am afraid not, Jan. That was not part of the KGB plan." Jan began to understand, at last, that he himself had been the object of two failed attacks by the Spetznatz team.

"And for how long have you known this, Galya?" he asked, sitting upright for a moment.

"Shall we talk about that tomorrow?" said Galina, reaching firmly for the light switch. "Do we ever know anything for certain in this sordid business? Let us work together now."

Jan gradually moved down her body, to the ample curves which had excited Victor Krasnov before, and were now Jan's to explore if he wished. He found they were ready to be exposed, and more than ready to be fondled, one by one in the dark.

This time Galina lay submissively on her back, so that he could gently inflame her most private fantasies and deepest emotions, before bringing her to fulfilment. The mutual joy which followed was pure and tender.

"Thank you, Jan, I will always remember this night," Galina murmured as the ecstasy took over her body and its myriad senses. Jan, too, was deeply moved, and realised he had fallen in love at last, for the first time.

CHAPTER 20

Near Calais

The sky next morning was almost black, and the air palpably moist, with a strong wind from the North Sea. A severe weather warning was issued for the Calais area and the channel coast.

At the European Commission the subject for the day was 'Subsidiarity of New Members', a debate to decide whether or not the countries of Europe would be allowed to decide their own futures, or be subservient to greater powers again. The quiet hum of air conditioners in the huge theatre kept out the real world and the worsening weather - terrestrial and political - outside the Berlaimont building. The Members' noses were for the most part firmly pressed against the mountainous piles of documents which they had just collected from their huge letter boxes before the debate.

Not far away near Mons, the fog of war was steadily descending on the Nato Council, which was meeting to discuss 'Operations in the Balkans', a topic guaranteed to keep the military hierarchy occupied for many months to come, at the taxpayers' expense. These expenses easily covered the heavy hospitality preceding and following each long drawn out meeting. The two alliances, European and Nato, could well be on the road to nowhere after the new Russian President had thrown most of the latest operational plans onto the scrapheap, but it did not really matter as long as the tills continued to ring up all expenses paid, and the huge salaries of the representatives kept on rolling in.

At the Calais Terminal, the new head of security, Phillipe Villeneuve, was in conference with Jean Moris, the Controller East, and others. The subject was 'Higher Security Measures - Plan Raphael'. There was no representative from Folkestone, an unfortunate omission which had its origins in the 19th Century rivalry between France and England, a competition still alive and flourishing to this day. The Director of Security opened the meeting:

"Good morning, gentlemen. This meeting is intended to update you on the latest state of security at this terminal. Several things have happened, of which you should be aware. Following persistent reports of a plot against the tunnel, inquiries in Belgium revealed that there was substance in this theory, and we are still in touch with the Mechelen Gendarmerie, who have been watching a house thought to be used by international terrorists.

"The evidence caused us to start searching nearer to Calais, because it is most likely that any plot against the tunnel would originate here rather than in England. You may recall that the British MI5 apprehended some I.R.A. terrorists and their huge lorry bomb some time ago. The same thing could happen here." Villeneuve paused. The audience was silent, and so he continued.

"Now for the latest revelations. We have been searching Calais hotels for a possible team of plotters, because we understand from the Mechelen Gendarmerie in Belgium that there is a link between their suspects and another group working here. I cannot be more specific at the moment, as there is insufficient evidence for the Gendarmerie to make any arrests, and the matter is still ongoing.

"We thought that we had found a suspect group at a hotel in Calais, but just as we were looking further at their alibis and movements they checked out of the hotel, and have not been seen since. They are three young and tough looking operators who claim to come from Latvia, but we now suspect that they are Russian. The leader is called Alain Delbois, which is obviously a false name, as they do not speak French, but Alain does speak some English. We are still looking for these people in the area, so far without success. Meanwhile, a state of extra security has been ordered at this terminal. I will ask the Controller to speak about that now."

"Good morning. As most of you know, Phillipe Villeneuve is our new Director of Security, on loan from the DST. He is in close touch with Groupe Diane, the Belgian anti-terrorist organisation, and has been studying the situation since we first heard of a possible plot against the tunnel, from our friends in the British MI6. As a result of recent developments, which Phillipe has outlined, I have ordered a review of security at the terminal and in the tunnel, to be known as Project Raphael. This has not yet been put into action, as I intend to coordinate your opinions and recommendations before issuing definite instructions to all staff here. I am sure that this will result in a better security plan, and I propose to implement any new measures that may be needed from midday tomorrow if possible. If the traffic had not been so heavy today, we would have preferred to start implementation today, even on a piecemeal basis, as the threat must be taken extremely seriously."

At the deserted farmhouse by the D940 road near Calais that afternoon, Alain's arrival was anxiously awaited by his two team members. There seemed to be occasional police activity on the main road which passed by 200 metres away, although it could have been routine.

Eventually, as the dark clouds racing past the trees bordering the farmhouse gave way to dusk, a white truck with the gold and red markings of the Stella Artois brewery turned left off the D940 and, with its sidelights only showing, lumbered down the track to the house. It stopped out of sight from the main road, behind the old farm buildings. Alain and Jan climbed out stiffly after the long drive from Leuven.

Bernard was waiting and watching from a window, Charles was in the main room setting up a gas light. Alain spoke briefly to his second-in-command.

"Bernard, I intend to go ahead with the mission today, as weather conditions are ideal. Where is Charles?"

"He is inside, fixing up some lights."

"Then stop him. I do not want any lights to show here. Both of you must come to the vehicle now. There is no time to waste. I am certain that we are not safe, even here: it is now or never."

Jan recoiled at the thought of the mission starting with so little preparation. He still had to finalise his own private plan, which needed to accommodate his SVR chief, Galina Svetlov. Perhaps this haste was the Spetznatz way - bravery to the point of foolhardiness, leading either to spectacular success or resounding failure, like the hopeless Cossack charges against the German tanks in 1941, when a whole cavalry brigade - as in Poland before - would be wiped out in half an hour of useless carnage. The battlefield tableau of Waterloo came to his mind. History had been repeated since then, and might be yet again.

"Now we will rehearse our movements," said Alain abruptly, as if his life was in danger - as it was. The other three huddled round his torchlight in the gathering gloom of a furious and stormy night. The wind had started, the rain was not far off.

"Today, the weather conditions are ideal. The ferries cannot move, and the tunnel will carry all the traffic. Security will be sacrificed to commercial considerations. We cannot hope for a better opportunity to carry out our mission. I want you to watch carefully." Alain climbed onto the vehicle with his torch, and spoke from a crouched position on top of the beer kegs.

"The bomb is positioned at five ten, which means five places from the left front and ten places to the rear. It is one layer down in the stacks. I will set the timer before we enter the tunnel. It has twenty-four main divisions, divided into half hours by smaller marks between the hours. So in ideal conditions it could be accurate to about fifteen minutes. However we can not rely on a clockwork mechanism for that, especially in the dark, so we must all work on thirty minutes delay, and not try to time it more accurately."

"OK boss," Bernard countered, "but what happens if we are delayed going into the tunnel? Surely there will be delays tonight, with all this heavy traffic?"

"We will decide on that when it happens," replied Alain. "I propose to stay behind in the truck when we go into the shuttle train, so that I can change the timer. As we go into the tunnel, it will be set for less than half an hour, because it takes the train only half an hour to go through the tunnel. You, Bernard, will come with me and Jan, and will both travel in the drivers' coach which is directly behind the locomotive. Charles, you will remain at the farmhouse, and report to our masters if we are successful. Now, we know how we are going to stop the train with our smoke grenade, I am sure."

Bernard replied. "Yes. I will be in the driver's coach behind the locomotive. As soon as we enter the tunnel I activate the grenade, and shout 'fire'. The coach has two Eurotunnel guards on board, who will stop the train at a platform, and we then go into the service tunnel."

"Correct so far, Bernard, but what did you miss out? Did you spot that, Jan?"

"We look for an ambulance or service vehicle to take us back to the terminal - is that what you mean, Alain?"

"Not quite. Remember, I am still in the shuttle wagon,

possibly 200 metres or more behind your coach. I have to reset the timer if necessary. You must make sure that the train is stopped long enough to enable me to get out. I will have to walk past several wagons before I reach the platform. So how will you keep the train in place for up to five minutes?"

"Obviously," Bernard replied, "we do not go to the exit yet, but wait for you to arrive. If necessary we complain of smoke poisoning, and ask for treatment by the first aid staff, who will have arrived in an ambulance through the service tunnel. Or if that fails, we ask to go back to our vehicle to collect something. Then we can make sure you are ready to get out of the train."

"Exactly. When you see that I have arrived, we three all get into the ambulance or service vehicle and are driven out of the tunnel. Is that quite clear?"

"That is assuming that everything goes according to our plan," Jan protested. "Suppose you are not allowed to stay in the truck, then we are all at the mercy of the bomb."

"Don't worry, I will set the timer again, or reset it, just before I get out of the truck," said Alain. "If I cannot stay with the truck, we stop the train and get out, just as we planned. The problem there is that the bomb will go off in fifteen minutes and our mission will fail if the train is reversed back to the terminal."

"Unless," said Jan, "one of us tells the tunnel staff that we need to board the shuttle wagon again to check our vehicle. I could manage a suitable explanation, I think, and at least delay the train." Jan did not really believe this, but perhaps Alain could be left behind on the train.

"That sounds a good idea, in case our original plan is not working," replied Alain. "Then any one of us could board the truck and reset the timer. But remember, we may have to change the plan when we get into the tunnel. And you Bernard, as my deputy, will be in charge if I am not present. Jan, you will do all the talking - is that quite understood?"

179

The two murmured their assent.

With that, Alain got down from the truck, and said goodbye to Charles. His torch beam seemed to have lost some of its power. "If we return, Charles, obviously we can get in touch with Control. If we do not come back, you should leave the area within twenty-four hours, by which time you will have found out the situation, and then report to Control. If there is a huge explosion, the same thing applies. Wait for a few hours for us to return. If we do not, report to Control, as they will expect to hear from you. Are you clear about that?"

"I think so, boss." Charles sounded as optimistic as possible in the darkness and strong wind, which rustled through the trees and made Alain's voice difficult to hear. Luckily his part of the operation was the easiest. "I will see you soon, I hope. Good luck. You are going to need it!"

Alain motioned to Jan, and they boarded the truck. Then Bernard climbed into the driver's seat, and drove slowly up the bumpy track to the main road before heading along the D940 towards the great terminal at Coquelles, which had awaited their final visit for a long time. By then, Jan was absolutely certain that Alain had been the assassin who came to the Kyrenia floating restaurant that night with the intention of killing him. He began to ponder urgently what his next step should be. The other two might have already decided to eliminate him at any convenient time. If he jumped out of the vehicle at the terminal, there was no chance of avoiding Alain's pistol a third time. He decided he would have to wait for a better opportunity, and try to turn the tables on Alain when they were on board the shuttle. Meanwhile he kept a nervous grip on his Browning automatic.

As they drove away from the farmhouse, Jan wondered what damage a nuclear explosion would do to the tunnel. He could see visions of a gargantuan waterspout of rubble and steam, pushed upwards by a huge white fireball. Then a rush of foaming water would pour into the tunnel, travelling at enormous speed and pushing everything before it, then it would pour into the service tunnel alongside, and from there into the second rail tunnel.

The train that he and the Spetznatz pair would be travelling on would be partly vaporised at the centre of the explosion, and the aluminium wagons melted as the heat travelled further down the tunnel. The drivers of the heavy goods vehicles would be killed instantly by the shock wave, and finally buried by a torrent of foaming chalk and water.

With the water level rising fast he could see no hope of escape for any passengers or staff in the other two tunnels. The eight hundred passengers in the approaching express train coming along the eastbound tunnel would find their train slammed into and pushed backwards by a wall of water, and would then be subjected to the horrors of the rapidly rising flood, turning their luxury transport slowly but surely into a submarine four hundred metres long, as they gradually drowned in a scene from hell, made worse by their violent and hopeless efforts to escape in the tumult and darkness.

Any form of rescue would be completely out of the question. The ambulance, fire and maintenance men and vehicles in the service tunnel would themselves be swept away within moments of the explosion. All would perish and be lost under the sea in the largest tomb ever created - stretching the fifty kilometre length of the tunnel that had been described as the engineering project of the century. They would have to stay there for months if not years, until a way could be found to drain and repair the tunnel, and to remove the twisted remains of the trains and the bodies of the drowned passengers. In reality, the tunnel might never be opened again.

CHAPTER 21

At Coquelles and Inside The Tunnel

The black sky was pierced by flashes of lightning over Calais as Bernard drove the truck towards the terminal at Coquelles. It seemed to him like a funeral procession as the vehicle edged forward in slow traffic. Chopin's Funeral March forced its way into his mind more and more insistently as he neared the final destination. The last time he had listened to that music was at the funeral of President Andrei Gromyko in 1988, and it had made a doleful impression then, but more so now.

Colonel Trimovich had his own private thoughts too. One which had troubled him for some time concerned his selection for this obviously suicidal mission. His mind went back to a scene in Kabul which would never go away: the desperate cries of the three rebels he had come to parley with and then kill, as they fought unsuccessfully for life while their headquarters burnt to the ground.

His orders had been vague, as might be expected during the collapse of the Russian attempts to master the dissidents before the civil war flared up again in 1988. General Malkov, then Colonel in charge of Spetznatz forces in Afghanistan, had ordered the youthful Major Trimovich to use his best efforts to obtain a local truce, but events had turned out differently, as often happens in war.

The use of the special forces in Afghanistan had brought little honour to the name of the Soviet Army there - an army which, during the much more desperate battle for Berlin in

1945, had shown amazing discipline and forebearance as it gradually overcame the defences street by street and building by building. Rape and murder had been relatively uncommon then, but such a stoic attitude was absent in Afghanistan, particularly in the key city of Kabul where chaos prevailed.

Trimovich had often wondered why, after the ignominious retreat of 1989, the head of Spetznatz never spoke to him about his conduct in the violent battle for Kabul. He had heard that Malkov hoped to achieve results by negotiation, and possibly a dramatic turnaround in the civil war, but this was hindsight and Trimovich had never been trained as a politician. Action was always in demand at the sharp end of battles; the higher command had gone soft as it always did when the chips were on the table. So Trimovich did his martial duty that night, and Malkov had to wait for his revenge.

The opportunity fell into his lap when he was suddenly ordered to provide a suicide squad for Operation Kingdom. He had no hesitation in selecting the well known Colonel Trimovich for his dash, daring and foolhardiness, and Trimovich had seized upon the appointment as an honour, until he realised it might be a one way ticket. Doubts were still lingering in his mind as Bernard swung the vehicle to the right and into the brightly lit, vast Calais terminal.

The enormous blue and white signs were everywhere in dazzling profusion, and easy to follow. None of the plotters had any knowledge of the heavy vehicle route to the train, but there was no going back as huge trucks thundered in behind them. The terminal was shrouded in a blanket of sea mist making vehicle outlines indistinct, and full of bustle as Bernard observed, rather quietly: "We don't stand much chance of crossing tonight with all this traffic. The ferries must have stopped sailing."

"That is exactly why I insisted on going tonight," Alain retorted sharply. "With all this traffic, they are bound to wave us through without a proper search. Jan, you have the export papers ready, I hope, and are confident you can persuade the authorities that we are just bringing the usual supplies of lager to the Folkestone terminal?"

Jan felt more confident now that he was apparently earmarked for survival. If so, the operation might be foiled more easily than had seemed likely when they started out. "It looks quite possible," he replied, thinking of his own rather than Alain's plan. "I don't think they will search the vehicle properly tonight - there will not be time."

"You sound a bit more cheerful now," joked Alain, not realising the reason. "Don't you think so, Bernard? He might even have qualified for the old Spetznatz if he had started thirty years earlier!" With that Alain, alias Colonel Trimovich, permitted himself the only belly laugh either of his companions could remember. Alain still saw himself as a dedicated, ruthless killer, and his profession had never struck him as offering much scope for humour. The job in hand always had to be done as expeditiously as possible and followed by a rapid exit from the scene of the mayhem. This mission was similar to many others, and perhaps simpler than some, even if it was on a grander scale. After all, as Jan had said, the vehicle was unlikely to be searched properly, and it was Bernard's job to pull the pin on the smoke grenade and ensure that the train stopped. He, Alain, only had to set the timer and walk quickly out of the doomed rail wagon - perhaps more quickly than he would have liked: he might even have to run this time. And he had his own smoke grenade to cover his retreat if things got nasty. His Makarov pistol, its trigger so lightly set to suit his quick aim and fire marksmanship, had ten rounds in the magazine, and that should be enough to dispose of anyone who got in the way. When Bernard pulled the pin on his smoke grenade, the HGV drivers might nearly die of asphyxiation, but the train would have to be stopped, and that was all that was required for the operation to succeed. The more smoke the better. Perhaps it might kill Jan, but that would be an advantage, as he would have to be disposed of sooner or later, to preserve secrecy. Even the loss of Bernard would be a small price to pay. Alain suddenly became more cheerful, a danger sign which the Spetznatz force had always warned against.

As the truck moved further into the terminal, the signs led straight on at first, and all vehicles were being waved forward urgently by guides with torches. Then came the first main diversion - HGVs were directed to the left on a separate path. The road wound round to the left and eventually to the right, finally turning into an immense marshalling area with white lines. Every lorry was stopped, nose to tail, for its first examination. An inspector walked up to Alain's vehicle, in the gentle rain.

"Good evening. May I see your papers, please?"

Jan stepped down, and handed over the export papers for his load.

"You are just going to Folkestone?" asked the inspector.

"Yes, we have a weekly delivery run to the British terminal."

"Strange, I have not seen your vehicle before. How long have you been delivering to Folkestone?"

"This is our first regular run. The demand for Stella Artois never stops increasing, it seems, and the restaurants at the terminal need a regular supply now, direct from the brewery at Leuven, in Belgium."

"I wish I was coming with you. Passport?"

Jan handed over his maroon European Community passport, with his photograph inside the back page.

"OK. You can go down this road to Exit 2, with the green sign. When you reach the walled enclosure with a red light, stop and wait for another inspector. You will not be kept waiting long, as we are very busy tonight. Try to avoid blocking the roads, and when you are waved on, maintain a steady speed to the next checkpoint."

Bernard moved the truck forward until it reached the walled enclosure, where the X-ray machine lay in wait. A ghostly blue light played around the area as a second inspector beckoned him into the foggy enclosure.

"Everybody dismount, please."

The three men got down from the cab, Alain trying to shrink into the smog and darkness, to make it appear that there were only two men in the truck.

"OK, now please keep your distance over there." The inspector pointed to a cubicle with thick grey concrete walls. Jan and Bernard went in, then Alain heard a buzzing sound as the vehicle was X-rayed. The inspector paused to look at the readings on his meter, then asked Jan what his load consisted of.

"Only beer barrels - Stella Artois lager, as you can see. Do you wish to have a closer look? We are delivering to the Folkestone restaurants. They have an enormous demand for lager over there."

"No, I can see that your consignment is properly stowed, and the scanner can see right through it. So everything is in order. Now go forward to the loading bridge area, where you will find the heavy goods vehicle signs leading to the shuttle train. Bon voyage!"

Jan was amused at the idea conjured up by the cheerful words of the inspector. The voyage was most unlikely to be anything describable as good. It was more of a desperate journey ending in a profound disaster, either for the free world or some of its less than free inhabitants, depending on whether the mission succeeded or failed.

The drive down to the train, helped forward at every turn by young guides waving torches and apparently just out of school - as some were - was soon completed without incident. Then the truck was beckoned onto the flat loader wagon, and

Bernard drove on into the first cavernous, aluminium HGV wagon with its perforated sides and open ends, then to the next, and slowly reached the rear end of the line of trucks, where a guide halted him.

"Please switch off the engine, apply the parking brakes, and leave the vehicle in gear. Then dismount and enter the amenity coach behind the locomotive. Ignition keys must be left in the lock, ready for emergency starting if that proves necessary. Welcome to le Shuttle. If you require any assistance, please let a member of staff know. Our journey time will be about thirty minutes."

Jan and Bernard got down from the vehicle, while Alain went to look at the load. The lighting was minimal, and he used his torch again to check the position of the bomb, lifting up a keg to reveal the timer. He decided to set the timer now, for thirty minutes, then he pulled out the red arming pin, well knowing that it was difficult to put back if the mission had to be aborted. Dr Jensen had only confided this information to Alain, to avoid causing alarm. The chips were down, in true Spetznatz style, he thought: from this moment on the tunnel was doomed.

There were still many empty spaces behind their truck, and Alain already knew it would take about ten minutes to complete the loading of the train, then it would be off. He spoke briefly to the others.

"Now you two must go to the coach. I will stay here for the moment, as planned. Bernard, you are armed and have your grenade, and I have one also. I hope to see you later, but it is essential that I am not incapacitated by smoke, so I will wait for the train to stop. Do not leave the platform area until I have arrived. By then, make sure you have the transport organised to get out through the service tunnel, by force if necessary. Good luck with your part of the operation - mine will not take long now."

In about ten minutes the train glided slowly and silently into the tunnel. In the drivers' coach the air conditioning could be heard quietly humming. Bernard waited only a short time before he walked to the back of the coach and sat down. He rummaged calmly in his shoulder bag, found the beige and green coloured grenade, and pulled out the aluminium safety pin.

The effect was dramatic. There was a scene of pandemonium as the thick grey, choking smoke swirled through the coach in a matter of seconds. The guards rushed to the intercom and one yelled to the train captain: "We have a fire in the driver's coach. Stop the train!" Then they turned to the seething mass of drivers who were cramming the approaches to the exit doors: "Everyone lie on the floor! *A planchet!*"

The train braked violently, throwing them onto the floor, and the coach doors on the right hand side opened onto a small, deserted platform. Most of the drivers ran out of the coach, coughing violently. A few lay still on the floor. Jan was by now at the front of the coach, and did not wait for Bernard. Instead, he grabbed one of the guards and shouted loudly over the din and hubbub: "Listen to me! There is a bomb on this train and it will go off in a few minutes. Come over to one side quickly - one of the terrorists may try to kill us!"

Then Bernard appeared close by, shambling groggily onto the platform, looking for Jan but held up by the mass of humanity still trying to get out of the coach. Jan shouted again at the train guard: "Listen, that is Bernard Engels, a Russian agent, but watch out - he is armed!" Jan dodged out of sight, but even in the smoke and noise Bernard heard his voice and drew his pistol, aiming at Jan to silence him for ever. Jan ducked behind another passenger, and Bernard's aim, affected by the smoke he had inhaled, was wide of the mark. The bullet just missed the train guard, and ricocheted off the tunnel wall with a sharp crack and a whine. The guard drew his pistol and shouted to Bernard: "Halt! Surrender!" The other passengers melted away, leaving the two to confront each other face to face. Bernard fired again, aiming at Jan who was crouching nearby, but hitting another passenger standing beside him. The other train guard fired a single shot, hitting Bernard in the throat and putting an end to the shoot-out. Bernard fell, bleeding from the fatal wound, and the guard picked up his discarded weapon, still smoking and hot.

"Now, you! Where is this bomb? Tell me quickly!"

Jan blurted out to the best of his ability, having breathed almost as much smoke as anyone: "It is on a truck carrying barrels of Stella Artois lager, about eight vehicles behind this coach. A white truck with gold and red markings. But hurry, we have no time to waste. The bomb has a timer which has been set! I heard the terrorists talking in the coach."

"Show me!" The guard gestured to Jan, to lead the way to the vehicle. "Quickly!" Together they edged their way swiftly through the shuttle wagons, alongside the line of trucks, a thin smoke swirling around them as they moved towards the rear of the train.

"Watch out, this man is also armed." Jan spoke quietly now, for fear of alerting Alain. When they got near the white truck, a familiar voice called out.

"Jan? What are you doing here? You are supposed to wait for me at the platform. I am leaving now."

Jan responded as best he could. "All is well, Alain. I came to say that we are waiting for the ambulance to arrive. Are you ready to come forward?"

"Who is that other person with you?"

"Nobody else is here. Now please come to the platform, or you will be too late."

Alain's feeble torch beam came to rest on Jan, then flicked briefly to the train guard following close behind in the darkness. Then with a Russian oath, Alain began to get down from the truck. Jan stayed where he was, his Browning pistol aimed at Alain.

"Stay where you are Alain, and tell me: is the timer set?"

"Of course it is. Now it is time for us to go."

"Before you get down" - Jan spoke with the unconcealed menace which had filled his mind for several days since he realised that Alain had attempted to murder him - "turn the timer to the end of its dial. We cannot succeed now. We are being followed by the train guards, who are armed. Surely you realise that the plan has failed."

"Jan, you are a traitor. I knew it. You will never find the timer. I have moved the barrels around. This is no time for talking. We must go now."

"Stay where you are, Alain. I will give you only a few seconds to do what I say," said Jan, switching on his own torch to blind Alain. Alain's shot rang out in the gloomy semi-darkness. Then he disappeared behind the vehicle.

At that moment the train started to glide forward, leaving all three in suspense, but in less than a minute it stopped in the cavernous French crossover tunnel, which was brightly lit. Alain's voice came from somewhere behind the truck.

"Don't try to fix the timer, Jan, or I will shoot! Get out while you can!"

Just then, the tunnel lights went out, leaving Jan and the train guard in complete darkness, to face the infamous Colonel Trimovich at his most dangerous, like a tiger deprived of its kill and ready to take revenge.

CHAPTER 22

Finale

The outbreak of a fire in the tunnel had always been the most dangerous eventuality, likely to cause a complete breakdown and possibly horrendous casualties. Hence Eurotunnel had carried out extensive exercises every month to circumvent the causes and effects of such a disaster, starting from the time that Queen Elizabeth Windsor and President Francois Mitterand agreed to open the new engineering marvel in June 1994, and - some would say bravely - to travel through the tunnel together, in the same shuttle train.

The tunnel had only just been licensed for passenger use by the two governments, after months of complicated trials, many unsuccessful, but use by Heads of State was still a gamble at such an early stage. A malfunction would have created very bad publicity for the tunnel.

Monthly exercises at both terminals had examined the possibility of a fire gutting the entire train, or smoke filling the tunnel as a result, killing all the passengers. These fire studies were held religiously, some would say to the detriment of all others, such as breakdown, collision or hijack.

The word 'Fire' was tunnel Police-speak for any occurrence of smoke, fire or electrical short circuit in the system, and if any of these happened red indicator lights flashed automatically, not only on the Train Indicator boards at both terminals, but also on the control and security computers. At that point the main programs on both control computers shifted from the general operating program to a different set of sub-programs, with a wide variety of options.

Although the Train Captain or Chef de Train was nominally in charge of the train, and the driver employed to take it from one point on the railway to another, as soon as the red lights flashed a different system operated. The Folkestone terminal remained in charge of the train and its movements as usual, and the Calais terminal was fed with information to enable it to take control if necessary. But nobody had been able, for practical reasons, to enter into the complicated control program software a complete combination of actions which might be needed to deal with the ultimate spectre of a total power cut and an effective terrorist takeover of the train.

A total power cut would of course mean that the control computers would crash and would have to be re-booted in order to re-start their main programs. Then they would have to exchange information all over again, to pick up where they had left off, before starting up once more the incredibly complicated series of computer operations which kept the tunnel and all its services functioning around the clock. But if the power failure took place after the system had switched to its sub-programs following a fire warning, the main program of control would not operate until it was re-started.

"Calais to Folkestone. We have a fire on board HGV Shuttle 13. As yet we don't know the cause."

"Folkestone to Calais. OK, we will maintain control. Please keep us informed."

"Calais to Folkestone. This is serious. Please alert your security staff and keep open all security channels."

"Understood."

"We are putting the Controller on the phone. Please attend."

This was not the only piece of Police-speak with two

meanings: one denoting action, the other a waiting role. George Trent picked up the red phone, a secure line reserved for the two Controllers and their deputies, to swap executive information such as the price of Nuits St Georges at Calais - a subject dear to George Trent's heart since he had taken over his joint Anglo-French responsibilities. An up-to-date knowledge of such matters was essential in this and many other Euro-appointments, such as the European Commission in Brussels.

"Hello, Jean, what is the problem?"

Jean Moris, the Controller East, replied calmly as was his manner. It might have to change soon.

"George, we have a small problem of a fire on board Shuttle 13. We have taken off the HGV drivers, but now there is a report of a bomb on board the train."

"A bomb?" George Trent's pulse seemed to stop for a moment, then raced to catch up. "We have not practised that recently, Jean. What do you suggest?" He played for time.

"I propose to put the whole train into the crossover tunnel on this side, to minimise damage. That is the best plan, I think." Moris was still taking the news calmly, and Folkestone was still in control.

"Good. You do that, Jean. We will take over the train movements, in case the driver is attacked, but will let the driver move the train to your crossover."

A few minutes passed by, then the secure phone rang again.

"George?"

"Yes, Jean?"

"We have a nuclear device in the tunnel, according to our informants. I have alerted our security detail to go into the tunnel. All are trained as marksmen, and we have the train stopped in the crossover. We are looking for a terrorist team who brought a bomb onto the shuttle, disguised as a barrel of lager coming from Belgium."

"Jean, my computers are jammed with information now. I think we are entering unknown territory. The system appears to be over-loaded. I am getting all sorts of error messages on my main screen." George Trent was privately devastated by the turn of events, but had regained his composure now. The problem was on the French side, not his.

"We are watching the situation, but I think we will have to take over control here," said Moris. "The problem is at our end of the tunnel, but the passengers are technically on UK territory, is it not? We do not have jurisdiction now, I believe."

"Jean, let us not worry about those technicalities now," Trent replied. "You and I control the tunnel. Do you think I should pass over control? Are your people ready to take over?" Trent spoke as coolly as possible. After all, it was a pleasant evening in England. The setting sun had painted golden colours on the control room windows, stars had begun to twinkle in the background, and the storm had not yet reached Folkestone.

"My people are still taking up their positions at the control centre. I think we will be ready in one or two minutes. Apparently there is a terrorist at large in the tunnel, but we are deploying our special forces to find him."

"Jean, I will have to push my red button if you are ready - we can't go on like this."

"George, I will send my special police force in from this end. The train is only five kilometres into the tunnel."

"OK, Jean. Will you do that as soon as you can? Now, will you take over control?"

"Yes, hand over now George."

The Controller West pressed the red button, but nothing happened.

"Jean, there is a power failure, according to our computers. Our screens have gone blank. Have you got the same problem?"

194

There was no reply.

A bolt of lightning had struck the circuit breaker at the Calais transformer, which was feeding the tunnel that day from the French nuclear power grid, putting the transformer out of action for a few minutes. The resulting shutdown of electricity to the overhead electric catenary line in the tunnel, and of all other current supplies to the terminals, from the control systems themselves right down to auxiliary lighting, had long been forecast. To reset the system, the Folkestone transformer had to be switched into the power lines temporarily, but only after a number of controls had shown that the reconnection of power posed no danger to any maintenance personnel sent to the stricken French transformer. The theoretical time for a reconnection was only five minutes, but a total power failure also shut off all the control mechanisms designed to help restore the supply.

While the emergency power generators were being switched on and fed into the dozens of control centres, to provide computing power and all the diverse functions of control, news of an attack on the tunnel reached the British and French security services. All government offices were of course closed by now, and remained unconcerned about the biggest threat to European security since 1938 and the Munich crisis. MI6, which had a listening watch, was elated when the news came through that evening, as their theories were completely vindicated. They would be able to express concern, but surprise that it had taken so long to track down the criminals across the water. The French DST was informed by Phillipe Villeneuve at the Calais terminal even earlier, and were infuriated to know that the close search they had mounted in the Calais area had narrowly failed to avert the catastrophe. Both secret services maintained a watch and waited for further news as the night wore on. Luckily Jean

Moris kept cool and did what was required of him.

In the tunnel, the lights had been out for several minutes. Jan Brouwers managed to climb aboard the truck bearing the enormous bomb, aware that an explosion could come at any time. The train guard stayed with him as he searched for the timer. Then a voice came echoing out of the darkness.

"Jan, one more move and it will be your last. I am watching you. I can hear every move you make. I am just behind you."

In the inky darkness, it seemed quite possible. But it had been obvious that Alain's torch was failing, so how could he see? Nevertheless, Jan was sure, as he felt in the dark for the timer, that the end of his world might be near. He moved aside for a moment.

"Alain, listen to me. Galina told me this is only a practice run, not the real thing. Turn the timer on, and we will both escape."

"I don't believe you, Jan. We are not both going to escape, only one of us." The voice seemed very close but was muffled by echoes, so it was impossible to tell where it came from. "Jan, if you try to reset the timer you will die."

Suddenly the lights came on again, to reveal Alain standing on top of the beer kegs. Jan took a wild shot with his Browning, shouting: "Get out, Alain, or you will be the one to die!" The boot was on the other foot now, and Jan was the assassin this time.

The train guard took aim beside him, and Alain could be heard scrambling down the far side of the truck. The train guard called to him: "Come out of there, or I will fire!"

The response was silence.

In the next few moments a team of marksmen which had boarded the train from the cavernous crossover tunnel arrived close to the desperate standoff. Jan felt secure enough to climb aboard the vehicle. Looking around nervously he could see nothing to threaten him, except the constant knowledge that the bomb might explode at any minute. He guessed what that could do to the train and the tunnel. He lay on top of the barrels at position five ten, and lifted the upper keg. There, underneath, was the timer, illuminated in his torch beam, with only a few minutes left on the dial. He turned the dial clockwise fully, and then, with a groan of total weariness, climbed down limply from the vehicle. Instead of the train guard, who had gone forward to meet the sharp-shooters, he came face to face with his old assassin in the semi-darkness.

He shone his torch into Alain's face as he pointed his weapon. "Alain, I can get you out of here. We are not going to blow up the tunnel. This is an exercise, as I told you. The bomb is not real. It is only a practice device this time. Your masters in Moscow have been trying to put an end to your career. This is their way."

"Jan, you are a traitor. We must say goodbye now."

Both men fired at the same moment, but the result was two bullets bouncing off the aluminium sides of the shuttle wagon with the sound of metallic thuds. The shadows were too deep to aim accurately, and both men were exhausted now. Jan's shot had grazed Alain slightly, but Alain, blinded by the torchlight, had missed completely.

Then the sharpshooters were on top of them.

"Everyone, stand still!"

Jan had heard this before, in the floating restaurant, and he obeyed instinctively. Alain slid out of sight in the darkness behind the truck, his shadowy face twisted with the misery of his final failure, and of the physical pain he started to feel.

"Who are you?" shouted a fierce looking soldier of the French Frontier Police to Jan.

"I am on your side!" Jan yelled back in the echoing tunnel confines. "I am trying to stop a terrorist from the Russian special forces blowing up the whole train and the tunnel!" Jan did not give his name: he intended to get away before any more awkward questions could be asked. "Please, get the train out of here. I have stopped the clock which is connected to the bomb." The train guard came to Jan's defence, and confirmed what Jan had said. "This man is right. You have arrived just in time. It was the terrorist or us. My friend here has saved the train."

"Where is the terrorist?" shouted the Police team leader.

Jan answered wearily: "He has gone towards the back of the wagons. We must move the train on to Folkestone. Can you stay here in case this maniac returns?"

"Yes, but we intend to find him before we move on."

"No," the train guard insisted. "We have to go on to Folkestone quickly. The next shuttle will be coming soon. We are running late, and the traffic is very heavy. We must move the train on!"

"Wait, I will send two of my men to look quickly at the rear of the train, to see if we can find him. Tell the train captain to wait a moment."

The French security team vanished in the semi-darkness, but were back in a few minutes. "There is nothing to be seen. We had better go on. There is nothing more we can do."

The train slipped away quietly, and soon emerged in twilight at the Folkestone shuttle platforms. The drivers had already arrived through the service tunnel, and started to unload their vehicles noisily. The two train guards turned to Jan briefly.

"We don't know who you are, but you deserve a medal - except that we do not give such awards in France!"

Jan smiled grimly. Such a night could never be repeated. He was thinking of meeting Galina in Brussels, to live again. He thanked the guards for their help.

"I must go now, but thank you for what you did to stop the terrorists. I have no idea who they are, but you saved my life!"

Jan did not elaborate or wait any longer, except to warn

the train guards that the bomb appeared to be set for twenty-four hours, and there seemed to be a red safety pin which must be put back. They wanted to ask more questions, but were too busy with their other duties, and it was Jan's turn to disappear from sight in the bustle and drama of the train's arrival at Folkestone.

The shuttle was soon unloaded, but Jan stayed on board. Then the train went into the underground track which turned it round and brought it back to the loading platform for its return journey. A few minutes later it left England and took him smoothly back to Coquelles without any further problems. The fate of the Stella Artois lager and its export papers no longer concerned him - they would have to reach their destination without him. The export documents were not really in order, but he was free at last.

At the back of the terminal, the Terminator was waiting for its next victim - twenty thousand litres of Belgian lager.

CHAPTER 23

Epilogue

The official inquiry into the whole affair took a long time to complete. There were very few witnesses who could tell the story coherently, and those who tried were for the most part bound to secrecy, so the results were never published. Jan Brouwers would have been invaluable, and might have been put on trial for his part in the plot, but he was never identified as a member of the terrorist group, and consequently never found out, to the relief of the new Russian government.

The inquiry discovered that the bomb had been live and of very low nuclear yield, but sufficient to destroy the tunnel by flooding, and all nearby equipment, trains, passengers and operating personnel if the weapon had exploded.

Bernard was identified when Phillipe Villeneuve got in contact with Inspector Bonchance, who instantly recognised the body as one of the three men he interviewed at the Hotel des Bains. Then a body found in the tunnel next day was identified as 'Piotr Trimovich' by the plastic disc he had been wearing around his neck before he was decapitated by a train. Again Bonchance was able to pinpoint him as another suspect he had already interviewed.

At first the discovery of the plot was hushed up, to avoid panic and a catastrophic drop in Eurotunnel revenue, which would have closed the tunnel just as surely as the bomb. Later, in a diplomatic representation to the new hardline Russian government, a request for help in tracing Piotr

Trimovich's identity and finding the rest of the plotters was met with a firm denial of any knowledge or complicity in the events described. A similar request to the Belgian government received an equally sharp response.

The obvious simplicity of the plan, and the fact that it had so nearly succeeded, fuelled a press witch-hunt when the inquiry was inadvertently leaked by a civil servant. An appeal by Eurotunnel to the British and French governments to fund the replacement of the old computer systems which controlled the tunnel, so that both were compatible, met with a more positive response this time, so Project Brunel finally came to be funded. Although the new American gas-powered locomotives were still not available to carry out pollution-free rescue work, five were ordered, and a completely new computer system was installed at the two terminals, vastly superior in speed and power of control in all foreseen circumstances. An independent backup supply of electricity to all computer systems was provided under the project, so that they could never go down at a crucial time, and handover procedures were tightened up at both terminals. Possession of a valid European Community passport was made mandatory for all HGV drivers and their crews entering the Shuttle, and surveillance methods were radically improved.

A new decoration, the M.E.O. or Member of the European Order (Membre de l'Ordre Européen or M.O.E.) was instituted by the European Parliament, and awarded for the first time to the two Controllers, George Trent and Jean Moris, in recognition of their part in preventing the destruction of the tunnel, which was cited as a model of European cooperation. This soon earned the soubriquet on the British side of 'My Efforts Only' and on the French 'Membre de l'Ordure Européen'. Ordure can be translated as trash or rubbish: the Revolution of 1789 still influences French thinking.

MI6 and the French DST received no formal recognition

for their vital work, as would be expected, nor did the retiring Jan Brouwers. To guard against reprisals from the SVR, Jan changed his name and moved to the Brussels area. He duly married Galina Svetlov at a church fit for heroes, the small and beautiful, thousand year-old Sint-Niklaaskerk at the Grote Markt, just off the Grand Place, and both are working for the Belgian intelligence service.

Ken Johnson, whose persistence led to the chase and eventual hounding of the Spetznatz operators from their hotel at Calais, and their precipitate operation which failed owing to lack of adequate preparation, was promoted and was eventually able to retire with a good pension, and look himself in the eye more cheerfully in the bathroom mirror.

Allan Gunn, a frustrated bachelor, finally married his faithful secretary, Sally Strang, and was promoted Head of Section. He still lives a stressful life in an otherwise quiet suburb of Surbiton.

Phillipe Villeneuve, although not considered senior enough for the award of the new European Order, was also promoted for his work in pursuing the plotters and helping to save the shuttle train.

The KGB and SVR destroyed all records relating to the operation, as did the Russian Defence Secretariat, and the new President issued a Cosmic Secret order forbidding any further work on plans to destroy the tunnel. "We could do it at any time, it is so easy," he is reported to have said at the time.

THE END

An Engineering Colossus

A brief history of how the Channel Tunnel,
voted by engineers the greatest achievement
of the 20th century, was built

HISTORY

The first tunneling attempt was made at Shakespeare Cliff, about eight kilometres from the present UK terminal, in 1880. Work was stopped owing to fears of a French invasion.

The second attempt started in 1974, but was stopped next year as costs escalated. Part of the second excavation of 450 metres was used in construction of the present day service tunnel.

In January 1986 Prime Minister Thatcher and President Mitterand, whose father had been a stationmaster, met at Lille and agreed to back a third attempt. The following month they met at Canterbury to sign a treaty, promising no public money for the project.

The following year the French and British Parliaments gave their assents, and an Anglo-French treaty was ratified at the Elysée Palace by the two leaders in July.

On the British side work began in November 1987. Almost immediately water and rock started to pour into the excavations. Morale fell and progress was almost non-existent. The project appeared to be in jeopardy - a popular press headline read: 'The Chunnel may not be finished'. The work was one year behind schedule at current rates of tunneling. The lending banks withdrew finance and work stopped. The Bank of England had to intervene, and a change of management was demanded. Then two outstanding American engineers were called in to manage the project, more equipment was introduced and the problems contained. Work speeded up dramatically, but costs had escalated. Nevertheless the lost time was gradually made up, and the project brought back on schedule.

Work started on the French side in February 1988, and ground conditions at Sangatte were also difficult, but flooding had been anticipated and special seals incorporated in the tunnel boring machines, so work was not held up.

In December 1990 the British and French tunneling teams met under the Channel as their two sections of the service tunnel were joined together, with great acclaim and celebrations. The two countries were physically reunited after 12,000 years of separation.

In 1991 the North and South train tunnels were completed in May and June respectively. World tunneling records had been broken, and the work completed a few weeks ahead of schedule.

The first train crossing took place from England to France in July 1992.

TUNNEL STATISTICS

The total length of tunnels built, including the central Service Tunnel, was 81.9 kilometres (50.9 miles) by the British and 64.3 kilometres (39.9 miles) by the French.

Width of the rail tunnels is 7 metres (23 feet) except at the two crossover tunnels which allow trains to change tracks. These are 156 metres (512 feet) long, 18.1 metres (59 feet) wide and 9 metres (29.5 feet) high.

On the British side ground levels had to be raised up to 12 metres (39 feet) by pumping over 2.5 million cubic metres of sea sand through pipelines. On the French side, owing to difficult ground conditions, a huge vertical shaft had to be excavated at Sangatte to gain access. This measured 55 metres (180 feet) wide and 65 metres (213 feet) deep - large enough to fit in the Arc de Triomphe. All the tunneling equipment had to be lowered and raised by cranes of 430 tonnes capacity.

The eleven tunnel boring machines were laser-guided, and the largest, with its spoil loading equipment and concrete segment placing machinery, was 180 metres (590 feet) long. On the British side the spoil was used to extend the coastline by 29 hectares (73 acres), on the French to fill in a large hollow - the fractured chalk marl was churned into a paste and pumped away through pipes.

The tunnel lining is by precast concrete segments, manufactured on both sides of the Channel to an accuracy never before attempted. On the British side the granite came from Scotland, and a crushing strength almost double that required for a nuclear reactor was achieved. Altogether 700,000 segments were required, of 94 different types. There is enough reinforcing steel to build several Eiffel towers.

The rail tracks total 200 kilometres (125 miles) in length and are continuously welded. They rest on 334,000 concrete blocks at two foot longitudinal spacing. Most sections of track were preformed in 180 metre (590 foot) lengths and installed by special rail gantries spanning the track.

The three tunnels are cross-connected by maintenance passages every 375 metres, and each is 3 metres (10 feet) wide. In addition the rail tunnels are connected by pressure relief ducts every 250 metres. These cross tunnels were all excavated by hand.

The Channel Tunnel is 50 kilometres (31 miles) long, and ends in France near Sangatte, where Louis Bleriot took off on his epic 30 minute flight to Dover in 1909. His crossing time was roughly the same as that of the present day Shuttle train.

The Tunnel is the second longest in the world, exceeded only by four kilometres by the Japanese Seikan Tunnel, completed in 1985, which connects mainland Honshu to the northern island of Hokkaido. Japanese technology was subsequently used in the design and construction of the tunnel boring machines for the European tunnel.

THE TRAINS

Besides freight trains arriving from Ashford in Kent and from Lille, tunnel traffic mainly consists of express passenger trains connecting London with Paris and Brussels, and Shuttle trains between Folkestone and Calais, carrying cars, coaches, caravans, motorcycles, and the heavy goods vehicles which travel on separate trains.

Express trains are about 400 metres (a quarter mile) long, and travel at speeds of up to 160 kilometres (100 miles) per hour. The express trains comprise 18 coaches seating passengers in pairs on opposite sides of the central aisle, and carry up to 784 passengers.

The shuttle trains are 800 metres (half a mile) long and travel at up to 140 kilometres (87 miles) per hour. They are of two types, tourist and HGV. The former can be single or double decker designs with solid aluminium walls, roofs and floors, and the single deck HGV wagons have perforated sides to reduce weight and dispel emissions. The shuttle trains have 28 wagons, plus the flatbed loading/unloading wagons at both ends in the case of the HGV shuttle.

The heaviest train is the HGV Shuttle, weighing 2,500 tonnes and requiring 7,700 horse-power. The approximate crossing times through the tunnel are 20 minutes for Express and 27 minutes for Shuttle trains.

All express and shuttle trains can be controlled automatically from either terminal in case the drivers are incapacitated, and have a locomotive at both ends in case of breakdown. In France the express trains reach 300 kilometres (186 miles) per hour and consume 14 megawatts of electric power.

POWER SUPPLY

Almost every function in the tunnels and trains runs on electric power. The system requires up to 160 megawatts to operate, equivalent to peak load for a small city.

The power is taken at 132,000 volts from the UK National Grid and 225,000 volts from the French. Both are transformed down to 25,000 volts to supply the trains and 21,000 for the terminals and tunnels. These voltages are again reduced to 400, 300 and 230 to supply the services.

The overhead catenary cables carrying power lines to supply the trains total 250 kilometres (156 miles) in length, and there are 950 kilometres (590 miles) of overhead conductor lines.

MAINTENANCE AND RESCUE

Five diesel powered locomotives are available for routine tasks such as shunting and maintenance, but also for train rescue. A disabled train could be pulled out of the tunnel by a pair of these engines, which discharge exhaust gases into special 'scrubber' wagons to reduce emissions in the tunnel.

The central service tunnel is used for access to the running tunnels, and is 4.5 metres (15 feet) wide. A fleet of diesel powered multi-purpose service vehicles provides fire, ambulance, police and maintenance services to the tunnels. A change of role can be achieved by changing the central container situated between the front and rear cabs. The vehicles can be driven from either end, but are designed to be controlled automatically by electronic means via signals from cables buried in the roadway. With a speed of up to 80 kilometres (50 miles) per hour, a service vehicle can reach any part of the tunnel within half an hour.

THE TERMINALS

Owing to the proximity of villages and ancient woodland the

UK terminal had to be kept as small as possible, and uses a circular underground tunnel to turn the shuttle trains round for their return journey to Calais. On the French side the ground was essentially wasteland, so there were no restrictions on space. Hence the French terminal is roughly the size of the whole London Heathrow airport complex, the British only the size of Terminal Four, about one fifth the size of the Calais terminal. The ten platforms at Folkestone are each 800 metres (half a mile) long.

To maintain clear tracks for through trains (express and freight) the shuttle traffic arrives at its platforms via four 300 metre (980 feet) concrete overbridges 20 metres (66 feet) wide which cross over the rail tracks and platforms. A further thirteen bridges were built at Folkestone to economise in space elsewhere.

Besides control and security centres, restaurants and administrative buildings, and transformer installations, both terminals have train maintenance workshops. Each terminal would formerly have been regarded as the largest construction project in Europe, but together with the tunnels they amount to the largest since the Great Wall of China.

FINANCE

The whole tunnel project was financed by 225 banks. As the initial revenues generated support less than half the interest payments at realistic market rates, the banks have recently studied a plan to acquire half the shares in Eurotunnel, and to reduce their interest charges. When the duty-free concessions given to cross-channel ferry passengers are abolished by the European Union in 1999, the ferry operators will have to increase their fares, and the tunnel will generate adequate revenue to cover its borrowings.

The cost of the tunnel project was originally estimated at £5.4 billion, but eventually over-ran its budget by nearly 100% owing to the difficult ground conditions and escalating costs of equipment and trains. The final debt has currently exceeded £9 billion, due also to equipment delays, the rising costs of railway equipment and the long time spent in commissioning trials to obtain a licence to operate from both governments. These trials covered the testing of 52 distinct sub-systems, which first had to be tested individually and then working together. The lost revenue from the summer of 1993, when the tunnel should have opened, increased the debt burden.

TRAFFIC

After a slow start, Eurotunnel has taken about 40% of all cross-channel traffic. In the first two years 2.5 million passengers and 183,000 vehicles were carried through the tunnels. In July 1996 240,000 passengers and 30,000 vehicles went through, and on one day - the last Saturday in July - 10,000 vehicles set a new traffic record. The Waterloo international rail terminal is now handling up to 3,000 passengers per hour, and the rail freight business is expanding. It seems that the economic hurdle has at last been surmounted, and profitability is in sight.

THE FUTURE

It is anticipated that a second tunnel will be needed early in the next century, and plans are now being drawn up. Eurotunnel, which has a 50-year concession, will be authorised to build it. The high speed rail link to London St Pancras will not be completed before 2002, owing to popular and planning objections: the Treasury is expected to contribute £1.5 billion towards the project. A major feature of the tunnels - the fibre optic connections between the two countries - will play a prominent part in communications of the future.

THE TUNNEL ENGINEERS - THE TRANSMANCHE-LINK CONSORTIUM

Balfour Beatty Construction Ltd.
Bouygues S.A.
Costain Civil Engineering Ltd.
Dumez S.A.
Societe Auxiliaire d'Enterprises S.A.
Societe Generale d'Enterprises S.A.
Spie Batignolles S.A.
Tarmac Construction Ltd.
Taylor Woodrow Construction Holdings Ltd.
Wimpey Major Projects Ltd.

This enormous Anglo-French partnership of engineering firms proved triumphantly that they could work together just as well as in opposition, to create the project of the century and a milestone in Anglo-French cooperation. No mention has been made, for reasons of space, of the many other outstanding engineering companies which built the trains and other state of the art equipment to run the tunnel, but many countries, including Britain, France, Italy, Germany, Switzerland and Canada made invaluable contributions on the way to setting the highest railway standards that have ever been achieved.